Our End Of The Block

P.J. Julius

This is a work of fiction. Similarities to real
people, places, or events are entirely coincidental.

OUR END OF THE BLOCK
First edition. September 15, 2023.
Copyright © 2023 P.J. Julius.
ISBN: 979-8-9891016-1-0

Dedicated to exuberance, joy, and laughter, and all those who seek them.

1

COLLATERAL DAMAGE

Ricky and I were crouched beside the big maple tree that was between Mrs. Wild's and the Barlows' back yards, trying to get everything set up without getting caught. The idea we were working with was simple, really. If you took a birthday candle, a bit of modeling clay and a firecracker and put it together the right way, you could light the candle and be long gone before it burned down to the firecracker's wick and set the thing off. The example scenario was for creating a diversion, but that's not what we were doing today, and we weren't using a firecracker. We had a bit of a modification to the original concept that we were putting to test. Instead of a firecracker, we had a bottle rocket.

I knew who had tied the pull-string firecracker to my front door, expecting it to blow up in my face when I walked out. The string firecrackers were like those party crackers where you pull the string and they go bang, only these had two strings and more bang. Unfortunately, I hadn't been the one to walk out the front door. I had gone out the back door and was in the Hoffmans' driveway bouncing a ball off the wall of our house. This was also the other side of my parent's bedroom wall, where my mom was laying down with a migraine which the ball bouncing wasn't helping. She had finally had enough and was going out the front door to tell me to knock it off, which triggered the string firecracker. It blew up right on her and her killer headache.

I was instantly grounded. I tried to deny it, but due to my past history with booby traps and explosives I was out of luck. However, I was pretty sure I knew who was responsible and I was going to make sure I got even, which is what we were working on.

"We could make a cone out of dirt." I said, scraping up a mound of loose dirt into a pile with my hands.

"Like a volcano?" Ricky was holding a stick over the ground trying to get a good idea what kind of angle we needed to get it to the back door.

"Yeah, but angle it that way …" I made a rough ramp shape in the dirt.

"I don't think so. Look how tall you'll have to make it, the candle would be all the way up here, too easy to see."

"We could camouflage it, there's all these leaves and sticks around."

"Maybe. But I think all that would catch on fire once that fuse lit. We don't want to burn down Mrs. Wild's yard, she's got nothing to do with this."

"Yeah true," I was looking around trying to find a solution.

"Hey, grab that brick. If we lean it on that we could set the candle next to it, it would cover the flame."

"Yeah. We have to anchor it somehow, too. Where are you pointing it?"

"Whaddya mean? That way." Ricky gestured towards the house.

"What if it hits the roof?"

"So? How many of these things have we put on roofs by accident? It's fine."

"Dude..." We had roofed bottle rockets before, like Ricky said usually by accident, and while I had no doubt it would take more than that to ignite your standard asphalt shingle roof, the Barlows' roof didn't look to be in such good shape. From the front it looked fine, but from where we were on the side you could see shingles curling up, and several spots near the back of the house had exposed wood. Any time there was a strong wind there would be shingles in the yard.

"What? Just lean it on there and get that candle lit and let's go." Ricky was anxious to get this set up and get out of there. I was too, but we had to be careful.

"We can't shoot at their roof on purpose," I warned him, "it doesn't look like it could take it. I want to try and get the door, like he got mine, not burn their house down. Besides, if this works, think of the possibilities..."

"Fine, just go low and that way then. Point it like this," he was adjusting the angle, "and if it goes wide and misses the door it will hit out in the yard or that fence. Maybe goes towards the alley, I don't know. These weeds are a pain in the ass anyway, I can hardly get a clear line through here."

The two back yards were like a display of extreme

contrasts. Mrs. Wild's was, appropriately, very overgrown, to the point of looking like some kind of prairie restoration project. There were little paths between the high grass and plants and stuff like game trails we had worn through during various adventures and short cuts.

Mrs. Wild was really old and not in great health. Often times me and the guys would find her outside looking for her cat Thomas, who had passed away about four years ago. We tried to be cool with her because the "maintain the property values" adults all kinda dragged on her, but at the same time they sure didn't seem to want to help her out much. We didn't have any problems with her, and we weren't pointing anything explosive at her house.

The Barlows on the other hand, in particular James Barlow, we had a big problem with, and that's why we *were* pointing explosives at their house.

While they seemed to have a scorched earth approach to almost everything, it was on clear display in the backyard, which was literally scorched earth in some spots. What grass was left was partially dead and in clumps. The rest was just dirt, except for their side of the big tree which was a little semicircle of woodchips left there by the previous owner. They always had dogs that were out tearing up the yard so there was absolutely no hope of them ever growing anything back there.

The current animal they had was a stray they had rescued. Last year they rented an RV and took a trip through the southwest, camping out along the way to Vegas. They returned with Pasha, a "stray dog" they had found in the desert. We were all pretty sure it was a coyote, based on the fact that it looked exactly like a coyote, plus it killed and partially ate a few cats and I think their other dog that we didn't see around anymore. We were told in no uncertain terms by our parents to stay the hell away from Pasha, but we had figured that out on our own.

I felt bad for Pasha the Coyote, and so did most of the other kids in the neighborhood, especially at night when she started howling. We understood her situation and could imagine it from Pasha's point of view. She was just out there in the desert doing coyote stuff, and then is essentially kidnapped by of all people the Barlows, although I guess if there ever was a family that was going to do something like that it would be them.

I had only been in their house a couple times, and it was different from any other house I had been in. There was no furniture in the living room or dining room, just cushions. The walls were covered floor to ceiling with mirrors that had gold and red accents, and all the archways between the rooms were painted red with gold accents as well. Were told that this was because Mrs. Barlow was a dancing instructor. It seemed reasonable I guess, but there was plenty of speculation throughout the neighborhood, primarily among the adults, that there was maybe a little more going on. No one ever explained it to us beyond that.

After you went through those two rooms towards the back of the house was the kitchen. It was a big open space, with windows along the entire back wall. There was a stove/range/grill thing under a hood in the center and all kinds of professional grade kitchen stuff. I swear there was a double up-and down oven set up that was the size of our refrigerator. This was all there because the oldest daughter Kelly wanted to be a chef. I don't know what other qualifications she had, but she definitely had the correct personality for it.

Her younger brother James was our age. He was in the same grade but not in the same class as either of us at school. James was the one who tied that firecracker to my front door, and that wasn't even the worst thing he had done to me, or any of us for that matter. He always had a mean streak in him, and maybe we were able to look past it because it hadn't been aimed at us, but that had changed. I'm not really sure when the shift started, maybe it was last summer? He started hanging out with some older dudes, and now we didn't hang out anymore. In fact, we didn't even see him all that often, and when we did it was usually unpleasant, him talking down to us, bullying, threatening, and pushing us around in front of his new friends, especially the younger kids.

It wasn't always like this. We used to ride bikes together, sometimes around the trails in the woods, and James would find the gnarliest hills and the highest jumps and hit them as hard as he could, leading to the occasional broken wrist or arm. This did not faze him. Once he jumped off the roof of their porch and broke his leg, and the fact that he didn't break both legs made the jump a success in his view. He really was a fearless rider though, and he was fun to ride with.

He had blond hair that was perpetually under painter's caps that had band names on them. I think this was also part of whatever he was going through, because he had started to change his jerseys and shirts from BMX gear to metal bands. I noticed he had pierced his ear and wore a little dangling fang from it now when he walked down to where I was bouncing my ball off the front steps one afternoon. He stepped in front and grabbed the ball, threw it up onto the roof of the house and walked back towards his house without saying anything.

The odd one out in the family was Amy Barlow, the youngest. She was in my brother's class in school, and according to him was quiet and a good student. It's almost like all the normality and kindness in the family had been unevenly distributed, with one person getting most of it and the rest of them not enough.

So, Ricky and I were huddled up there in the overgrowth trying to set up this little timed charge with the bottle rocket, which we were aiming at the Barlows' back door, although this created a couple issues we were trying to work through.

With the firecracker set-up, once the thing blew it also destroyed any evidence - not disintegrated it but scattered it enough that it would be difficult to figure out what happened if there was any sort of investigation. We weren't sure if that was going to happen with the bottle rocket but had no way to know until it went off, so we moved past that to the issue of targeting, which was a bit more of a struggle.

It didn't take too long to figure it out. The bottle rocket was leaning across the brick we found, with the tip of the stick slightly in the ground and the birthday candle tucked behind and below. We lit the candle and headed back to Ricky's front porch so we were nowhere near it and also creating our alibi. Anyone looking could see we were out front. Perfect. Nothing to do now but wait for the bang.

Birthday candles are usually only burning for what, maybe two minutes? How long would half a candle take? Five minutes? Ten? These are good questions to consider, and we did not, although it wouldn't have mattered much because neither of us had a watch on.

We were tossing a little white and red plastic football that had an insurance company logo on it back and forth to each other across our front yards. We both spaced out a bit, getting lost in the rhythm of playing catch for a while. It started to seem like a very long while. "Did you hear anything?"

"Huh?" Ricky tossed the ball back.

"The thing – did you hear it go?" Bottle rockets were about as loud as firecrackers, so even though it was in the back, we should have heard it.

"No, I don't think so, did you?"

"No, I don't think so either. How long has it been?"

"Maybe 10 minutes?" Neither of us was good with timing, but it felt like ten minutes to me. "How fast do those candles burn?"

"Not sure. You think it went out?"

I was skeptical, but this could have happened. "Maybe. It's not really windy though, and the candle's behind a brick. Could have been a dud."

"Should we check?" Ricky held the ball and pointed towards the back.

"Let's give it like another like five minutes just in case and then yeah, we can go on the deck in back, should be able to see it from there."

We played catch for what felt like another five minutes and then went around the corner of the house, down the driveway to Ricky's deck. There was a double railing around it, and it was lined by big pine trees on the side facing the Barlows' house which was two yards over from Ricky's. We both peered through the railings.

"Can you see it?" I couldn't get a clear line of site through the overgrowth.

"No – there's too many weeds. It probably went out." We later learned that the average burn time of a birthday candle is around 25 minutes. It had not gone out.

"Should we go check?"

This question ended up being irrelevant. At that moment, the Barlow's back door opened, and Mrs. Barlow stepped out, calling for Pasha, who was out in the yard. We heard the distinct whizzing sound of the bottle rocket igniting and taking off. I don't know if it was our targeting that was off, or if the force of the rocket nudged it sideways or what happened, but instead of hitting the door it went directly into the area at the top of the back stairs, in front of Mrs. Barlow but behind Pasha, and exploded.

If you think dogs react poorly to fireworks, you should see how coyotes react. Pasha went straight up in the air, did a twisting one-eighty, then hit the ground and got as low as her legs would let her. I guess it was a crouch if coyotes can crouch. Then she did a frantic scuttling circle – probably scanning for further attacks, and apparently decided it was time to exit the area, so she took off for the stairs, aiming to get back in the house, barking and howling the whole time.

Mrs. Barlow, who had started screaming when the rocket first exploded and had just continued to scream, further freaked out the coyote by making two mistakes, the first of which was trying to calm it down by screaming *"Pasha calm down!"* over and over, and the second was getting in between her and the door. Pasha cleared the stairs and bounced off of Mrs. Barlow, who finally seemed to understand that the poor thing wasn't in a good spot. She was trying to both hold the door open and use it as a shield but lost her grip upon impact and went down. Pasha tried to get through but got sandwiched between the door jam and the door that Mrs. Barlow had fallen against.

Me and Ricky dropped down on to our stomachs on the deck. We knew that we were in deep trouble if it got back to us. We were probably both thinking the same thing - come up with something to talk our way out of it, unless James found out, in which case we were probably dead. It was hard to think clearly with all the action going on.

When we looked up, Pasha was back in the house. Mrs. Barlow must have gotten some of her composure back because she was no longer screaming at the coyote. She seemed to have decided who was responsible for this already and was now screaming at her son James.

"You little … I am going to … when I get my hands on you … how many times have I told you no more pranks, no more fireworks, no more of *this*.... *James....James Edward Barlow ....when I find you...*" and she went back in the house slamming the door behind her. It was quiet again. Ricky and I just looked at each other, laying there on our stomachs on the deck.

"We have to get out of here while we have a chance," I whispered.

"Yeah, crawl for the steps. Now." he whispered back.

Curiosity had been replaced with self-preservation, so we stayed low, got to the steps, down off the deck and into the driveway between our houses.

"Whoa…"

"Yah. I feel bad about the dog though."

"Me too. And his mom…"

"Yeah, that too …"

Somehow, we had successfully tested the idea, caused some minor chaos, and got away clean. There was a good chance we wouldn't even be blamed for it.

We were idiots to think that though, and a brick through my garage window two days later told us that James Barlow figured it out. It wasn't so much the window itself that was the issue, but the intent. He wanted that brick to hit our car which fortunately was not in there at the time. I'm not sure why this pushed us over the edge, but it did.

"Are you sure it was him?" Ricky was sitting in the driver's seat of the partially assembled Mustang Fastback in his garage. I was riding shotgun next to him. We went there a lot to work things out. It was his dad's car and we liked to sit in there and talk when we needed some privacy. Ricky always said that his dad told him one day it would be his, so we kinda just treated it like it was already and hung out in there whenever we needed to or if it was raining or whatever.

"First that stupid string bomb tied to my door, now this? C'mon man, who else could it be? I'm so tired of him and his BS. Any time he's around I get it somehow. He rubbed gum into my brother's hair, and my mom got mad at *me* about it and I wasn't even there. Every time it's just bad."

Ricky looked thoughtful, "I think he's been ambushing raccoons with rocks in the alley behind my house, although maybe he's just using the racoons as an excuse to throw rocks around back there. But he's never really done anything beyond trash talking to me – oh, except for that graffiti on the back of the garage that one time, although I thought it was a pretty funny picture."

"Your stepmom didn't."

"True." Ricky replied, staring out the windshield and going quiet. He had a profile sorta like Harrison Ford, only with a crooked nose from laying down a bunt incorrectly and feathered blondish-brown hair he kept neat with a comb that stuck out of his back pocket. He was a little bigger, a little stronger, a little cooler than me, but it didn't matter. He had been my best friend since not long after we moved in next door six years ago.

He and his stepmom though, not a good situation. It seemed to me like they always had a difficult relationship. His dad was a contractor of some type and was usually gone working six days a week, and Ricky's stepmom never had kids before, so I guess it wasn't going as she had thought it would.

I changed the subject back to James. "Anyway, don't forget he knocked Ant's little brother off his bike after he made a jump just because he didn't like that he was celebrating the landing. It was a big jump."

Ricky was shaking his head, "I know, but I mean … so he's a jerk. What are you going to do? I might be able to handle him, but I don't think you could, no offense. Like – how mad are you? I don't know … I don't think it's a good idea."

He was right. I would most likely get my ass handed to me in a one-on-one fight. I didn't want to fight though. I had never been in a fight that I hadn't tried to get out of first, and I don't think I had ever started one in a situation like this.

"I don't want to fight, but I do want to do something, and if it hurts him, I'm not going to be sorry, you know?" I said. It was an interesting situation. We could just let the garage window slide and call the whole thing even right there. We did shoot a rocket at his mom and dog, even if it had been sort of an accident. He had started it by tying that string bomb to my front door that was triggered by my mom, and it did kinda feel like at this point, things were pretty square.

This time though, our anger with James had been building with each crappy thing he did, and we were finally at some kind of breaking point. Also, we were maybe a little overconfident in both our newfound covert demolitions experience as well as a recently acquired fresh supply of fireworks. Somehow, we decided that what we needed was not de-escalation, but a better response. We were going to finish it. A garage window for a garage! OK maybe not that far, but we were pretty mad, we just hadn't quite found the correct method to express it.

"I just don't know that he's going to care all that much if we smash out their garage window. Like, what's it to him? It's not his problem. He doesn't care about it. It's just a window. He needs to care about it."

"True, true…" Ricky trailed off and looked out the windshield for a minute, lost in thought. Finally, he said "He keeps all his bike stuff in the garage too, right? Like that BMX racing jersey with the patches and pads in the elbows, and that nice GT racing helmet?"

"I think so yeah, at least he used to. Why? You don't want to try and get it do you?" That was a level of risk that I don't think I was ready for. James treasured that pro BMX gear even though we didn't see him riding very much anymore, and I didn't even want to think about what he would do if he found out we stole it.

"Nah, we could get killed over something like that. But we could mess up the garage and that stuff in it, like with a dye bomb like he used in Smedley's hot tub? Or maybe bleach? Or bust open a spray paint can and chuck it in? I don't know. I mean he was trying to mess up something in your garage, I think it would make the point."

I liked where he was going but didn't like those options. Liquid delivery was usually messy and complicated. You needed enough of it to make a mess and that was hard to deliver. I did like the idea of sabotaging the inside of the garage though. I liked it a lot.

Suddenly I had it. I knew what we could use. It was perfect. I needed to get to Deacon's, but that was going to have to wait until tomorrow. We had plans for today already.

2

CASH ONLY

Let me grab my glove, and I have to check my rocket supply real quick," I said to Ricky as I hopped the fence back into my back yard. "Actually, while I'm doing that can you see if you have any birthday candles around? We still have some left but we're starting to run low. How many bottle rockets do you have left?"

"A lot. Hansen threw in like four extra packs because I bought that gross off him and he didn't like having the loose packs floating around I guess."

All the good fireworks were illegal. That meant that all you could purchase legally, in a store, were sparklers, snakes, smoke bombs, and snap-n-pops, all of which sucked.

I'm sure that the lawmakers who passed this ban had the highest ideals of public safety in mind, but what they really did was create a lively and completely unregulated underground firework industry in our state every year that peaked around the Fourth of July. This was also

15

enhanced by the fact that all the states surrounding us did *not* have a similar ban, so all you needed was to know someone who had vague ethics, smuggling aspirations, and reliable transportation and you could get pretty much anything you wanted - from firecrackers and m-80's to roman candles (the good kind that blew up after they launched) and more serious mortar-launched, near industrial quality stuff.

For most kids, up until the age of maybe nine, all fireworks fall into two categories - stuff you go and watch in a show, and stuff adults light off before, during and after you watch fireworks in a show. As you get older, you start to hear stories of firework fights in cemeteries and local forest preserves, high school dudes having huge epic battles that last for hours, but they're more urban legend than anything you can actually visualize, much less imagine participating in. Then you get old enough to get a paper route, or start cutting people's grass, or shoveling snow. You don't have much in the way of life expenses, so it's easy to save. It was cool to be able to buy candy or toys or whatever you wanted without having to ask, and it doesn't take long to realize that maybe there are other purchase options – options that can't be found in stores. At least not stores in this state.

The first time someone opens the trunk of their car and it's full of every type of firework you can possibly imagine, and many that you've *never* imagined, all right there in front of you and for sale, is just one of those experiences you don't forget. Usually, the only limitations are the amount of money in your pocket and how much nerve you have for lighting things that could cause serious personal injury and/or property damage.

The bigger the boom, the higher the price, and if you had limited funds, which most of us did, you had to try to balance out your stash. Maybe get a few bigger boomers or specials, but enough of the regular firecrackers and rockets to keep the action going.

It wasn't even that big of a deal really. It seemed like everyone knew a guy, or knew a guy who knew a guy, who had fireworks for sale. No one cared how old you were. Sometimes it was just a matter of being in the right place at the right time. Not that long ago I was playing a game of running bases with Ricky, Matty and some of the other guys on the diamond at Taylor Park when a familiar station wagon pulled up. A husky dude wearing cop sunglasses got out, scanned the area, and then went around to the back and opened the hatch-style door. A couple other kids headed over, and even though we weren't going to be buying we still wanted to see what the load looked like, so we wandered over to take a peek.

In the back of the station wagon was a pretty good selection of the finest the state of Indiana had to offer. Well, maybe the finest the roadside stands in Hammond had to offer anyway. Rockets of all sizes, from little guys that were about the size of a crayon all the way up to the big boys that were toilet paper tube sized mounted on fat dowel sticks. Something called a "Blue Streak" that looked like a cruise missile on a stick. Roman candles that sizzled, roman candles that exploded, roman candles that were four feet long and shot twenty bursts. Packs, belts and bricks of firecrackers. Boxes of m-80s, m-100s, things that looked like and could well have been sticks of dynamite. There were a few ground displays – shoebox sized things that had one wick and would launch fountains and mini mortars and smoke for "nearly 2 minutes" according to the wrapper. Jumping jacks that exploded, whizzers and winged "bees" that spun around shooting sparks until they exploded.

Sadly, it was all off limits to me, Ricky and Matty.

The seller of all these pyrotechnics was Heavy T. Most kids just called him "T" but me and Ricky and Matty called him "Coach T." He was the assistant coach on Olsen Foods, our official league baseball team. He was also probably the biggest importer of fireworks in the whole town. I think the reason he drove a station wagon was because of the "extra" cargo space. He had removed the fold down seat in the back but left in the floor cover, creating an ideal combination smuggling compartment and display case.

It was my understanding that he only made one big run to Indiana and loaded up all at once rather than taking on the risk of multiple runs. I always imagined this as some covert meeting in a corn field or backroad or something like that. Handing over a bag of money, quickly transferring the goods from one trunk to the other, leaving at separate times. My secret agent fascination bled into everything. In reality, the Indiana border was maybe 40 minutes' drive and as soon as you crossed over there was like a whole fireworks mall. It was right off the first exit over the border. It was more like going to a farmers' market than participating in some kind of covert contraband connection.

What he got and where he got it didn't matter though, we couldn't buy from him. He refused to sell to anyone he coached. No exceptions. I guess I can see where he was coming from. He didn't need to have that kind of liability, plus there's the whole setting a good example thing as well, although he didn't seem to mind if we possessed fireworks, and he sure made no secret about what he was doing. He just didn't want to have anything to do with the transactional portion of it, and it was smart business. Besides, he could afford to be selective. Everyone knew he got the best stuff, had the most of it, and was available, so he never had an issue moving product.

Because we couldn't buy from T, we had to find alternative sources for our fireworks needs, which we had mostly already handled this year. It wasn't that big of an issue, but we always had to endure some additional hoops to jump through and the inevitable price mark-ups. Amusingly enough, our firework purchases were more often than not exactly like what I imagined Heavy T's as being - meeting up with some weirdo in the parking lot behind Sears on North Avenue, passing over some cash and getting an unmarked bag or box depending on what we were after. Make it fast, pay cash and no questions asked.

This year I had money saved up from a paper route that I recently quit because I realized I hated it. I did not like early mornings. I did not like having to rush. I did not like how newspaper smelled. On Sundays the papers were so heavy I would load half the route into my cart, and they would take the other half on the truck to the midpoint of my route and drop them there so I could reload and finish. It was hard, honest work, which made it incredibly unappealing for a budding secret agent/private detective/ninja that I imagined myself as. A recent rainy Sunday incident involving a "supplemental section" that added like a pound to each paper that caused my cart to tip over, twice, was the final straw for me. I was out of the newspaper business forever as far as I was concerned.

But the cash was nice, and now I wasn't too tired to spend it, so we loaded up. We had done pretty well considering we couldn't use Heavy T. Ended up connecting with an old Boy Scout acquaintance of mine named Hansen and the local Robin Hood, Pat Vizzone.

Hansen was a military fanatic who sold fireworks to support his own habit. He didn't go for much in the way of variety, he did quantity and volume discounts. You also had to listen to a lot of conversation (more like lectures really) about blast force and first strike capabilities and things like that, which were interesting at first but after a while I really just wanted to take my fireworks and go blow them off, not analyze and discuss their potential strategic value.

The other connection, which was more local, was Pat Vizzone. The Barlows were one thing, but the Vizzones were something else. They lived in a two flat like ours. There were three in a row at the end of the block and then one around the corner that ran behind our back yards next to the alley, that one was the Vizzones' place. The backyard was brick and pavement and beer cans mostly. They also had a roll-off dumpster that we had high hopes for when it was dropped off. Perhaps they were getting ready to move, or maybe going to clean out the yard and garage at the fundamental level it needed.

That dumpster had been there for two and a half years now and all that ever happened was that sometimes they would have people over and have a campfire in it, and sometimes Pat Vizzone would set up empty beer cans at the far end and shoot arrows at them with a compound bow that was so powerful it would occasionally punch through the dumpster wall and bounce off the wood fence, or just go out into the front yard and sometimes the street if they missed the fence. It was insane, but totally in character for them and none of us were surprised or really even bothered. We just knew to go the long way around if Pat was out in back drinking beer just to be safe.

We could never say for certain who or how many people lived there, but there were some regulars. Like I said, it was a two flat, and we knew Mr. Vizzone, first name Tony, lived on the second floor with his wife and two daughters and Pat. Ma Vizzone, who we assumed was Tony's mother, was on the first floor. She was Mrs. Wild's competition for "weird old lady who should have had someone helping take care of her," and the competition was fierce.

While Mrs. Wild would be seen with her wig on crooked and possibly wearing winter boots with her summer dress, Ma Vizzone still did her makeup and hair, possibly in total darkness, but certainly without the benefit of mirrors and fully functioning eyesight. Sometimes her eyebrows would be up on her forehead near her hairline. Lipstick not only on her lips but around them, frequently making her upper lip a solid red or pink. She favored ponytails on each side of her head, and she had long gray hair so she could make that happen, but it was incredibly unnerving for first timers in the neighborhood to see what from the back looked like an older lady with her hair pulled to the sides only to have her turn around and see the crazy clown makeup. We felt bad for her and always tried to make sure she got home if we saw her out. Mr. Vizzone was always grateful and nice to us about it.

I don't know for sure what Mr. Vizzone did for a living, but that wasn't unusual. We were kids, unless someone was a fireman or an astronaut we didn't care. I couldn't even say for sure exactly what my own dad did. The neighborhood of course had multiple theories, most of them sketchy and criminal. Also, impossible to verify or prove incorrect. He was an enigma. The most solid information we had came from someone who fell into conversation with Tony after church one time, and that was that he was involved in trucking/supply industry somehow, worked a constantly shifting schedule and was on the phone a lot. This still seemed suspicious, but the most likely and the least farfetched anyway.

The kids were equally hard to define but fell into a younger/older segment. I could not say for certain how many kids they had, but we went to school with the youngest, Stacy, who was in second grade and walked with us sometimes. I know there was an oldest sister Marjorie, then oldest brother Pat. These two were out of high school – not saying graduated, just not there anymore – and could drive and had cars so they did something for money, although what that was we never saw or discussed with them. There were some pretty mean rumors about what the girls did for money but most of us disregarded them as gossip.

Outside of them, there were random people there. Usually looked to be young adult aged, or at least older than us, sometimes there for a bit and then we didn't see them again, sometimes longer. One time a cousin stayed for the summer; she was really nice. I think there was also the boyfriend/girlfriend temporarily staying there too. Like I said, it was a rather fluid situation and hard to keep track of, but we didn't think of it as a big deal.

For us, the Vizzones were both an aspiration and a warning. They were also the only people the Barlows, especially James, seemed to respect and were somewhat afraid of, so that should tell you something. The police were there often enough that it wasn't a strange occurrence. Sometimes it was a low-key roll up and sometimes several squads with lights rolling. Usually Marjorie was screaming at someone, and Tony would come out and talk his way out of it. No one ever left with the police that we saw, and the police always ended up leaving so it's hard to say exactly what was going on.

Pat Vizzone was Billy the Kid as far as we were concerned. He was clearly on the opposite side of the law, but we didn't see him as a bad guy. He wasn't very big, but we had seen him in fights, sometimes right out there in the alley, and knew he could handle himself. He was always calling us from the end of the alley when we were playing in Ricky's back yard to give us stuff that had "fallen off the truck" where he "worked." Ice cream sandwiches from a box of like 50. Cookies and bags of chips that clearly belonged in a vending machine. Once he gave us big bags of rubber bands. I'd like to think he did this because he was a chill guy who liked us, but we knew it was his way of buying our loyalty. We never talked when asked about him, not to teachers, parents, or the police. "No idea nope haven't seen him around. I think the last time I saw him was at church this past Sunday."

It was no surprise that Pat Vizzone had fireworks. What was a surprise was both the quantity and quality he had this year. We had already stocked up, and what we couldn't get from Hansen we got from Vizzone, but it was an interesting coincidence that we bumped into him as we were heading through the alley to cross the street.

"Hey man!"

"Hey little dudes."

"Ready for the Fourth?"

"Oh yeah. Are you? You guys need anything else?" Pat did not have the same ethics that Heavy T did and would sell us pretty much anything as long as we had the money.

"We are pretty well covered on the basics, but you got anything cool left? I still have a couple bucks."

"Step into my office boys…" Pat said.

Business concluded, and a quick detour back home to stash our purchase in the garage, we headed back out through the alley and across the street.

3
HOTBOX

I was on the mound, and Ricky was crowding the plate we had drawn in the dirt – like practically standing on it. He was doing it on purpose, and he stuck his butt out and shook it at me. I had no choice now. I went into the windup and threw it straight at his ass, not even trying to get it near the strike zone. The beanball hit its mark, and Ricky went down screaming, "You broke my ass oh it's bad…" He rolled on the ground for a second or two and then lay still.

I walked in to where he was motionless on the ground, picking up the rubber ball that was laying there on my way. "You want me to get your mom?"

"No, get *your* mom for me, will ya?" Ricky was laughing and started getting up.

"Don't crowd it or I'll come inside on you again."

"Maybe I'll hit leftie so I can have matching bruises."

"Up to you, but I got worse control on that side so I can't promise anything."

"Are you guys going to talk it out or can we get back to the game?" my brother yelled from the outfield.

"*Shut it!*" We both yelled at him. He gave us the finger as I walked back to the mound and Ricky dusted himself off and picked up the bat again.

If you hopped the fence into the Hoffmans' back yard, then cut through to the alley past the Vizzones' place and crossed the street you were in the baseball field behind Emerson Elementary school. It wasn't very big. There was only space for one diamond, but it had a back stop and an infield, so good enough, but we weren't using it today. We were all the way on the far side, against the back wall of the school.

Baseball was it for us, and if we couldn't play a game somewhere we were always playing catch or running bases. I spent plenty of time by myself throwing a ball at the concrete front steps of our house or bouncing it off the side wall and fielding whatever came back. I could (and did) do that for hours. I'm not sure exactly what the appeal of a ball being caught with a glove is on a psychological level, but it's there. We were too young for full-time jobs and too old for like summer camps or whatever so at some point during almost every summer day we got in a little baseball. We were all in the "official" village league and had games and practices and all, but that was organized with uniforms and equipment and schedules and all that serious business. That was great, but we liked to play without the structure, too. We had the time, and it was fun.

Ricky had backed off the plate a bit, looking like he wanted to get a solid swing on the next one, giving me a little space to work with. He was going to get me eventually, he was a better hitter than I was a pitcher, but I was still going to try.

"How about the old number one? Right here is good." He was wagging the bat towards the bottom of the zone. Number one is a common catcher's sign for fastball.

"I think the location on that last number one was pretty good, maybe I'll go there again." I replied.

"I'll charge the mound... *and then I'm coming out there.*" He yelled. My brother had started doing a little booty-shaking dance out in the outfield.

Ricky squared up and stared me down.

Windup and pitch, and I knew as soon as it left my hand that it was not where I wanted it, but right where he wanted it.

"good-*BYE*" Ricky said as he took a perfect swing, sending the ball sailing out over my head.

He was right, I turned in time to see my brother stop running as the ball went over the fence.

"One time I will stop being nice and go for your head."

"Haha that's probably what you wanted with that last pitch, but you got no control on this side of the box either."

In order to field a full baseball team, you need nine people per side, eighteen total. While there were a lot of kids of various ages running around the neighborhood, it seemed like we never really had enough players around at once to play a full-on two team game. You could make do with a few less, like maybe only 2 outfielders, right field was automatic out, and each player kept their own score, but that was still at least six or seven kids. Or sometimes one kid would just play pitcher and we'd all take turns batting and fielding. But that was also a bit of an issue.

In our heads we were Nolan Ryan or Goose Gossage, but in reality none of us were exceptional or even promising. None of us pitched for our league teams. I had heard that some of the Northside kids had private coaches, played for travelling teams and were being scouted (allegedly) but we didn't have any of that. We had the Johnny Bench fundamentals TV show on Saturday mornings sometimes, maybe some books from the library and whatever we learned from each other, our dads, and our league coaches. My friend Paulie could pitch, but he lived in a different neighborhood, so we only played together when it was official, for Olsen Foods.

"Ok ok. So you're at three runs, one out. Get back in there."

"Four runs. I had a man on first."

"What?"

"You hit me; runner takes a base."

"Oh, yeah right. Four runs, one out."

My brother had hopped the fence back into the field after retrieving the ball and throwing it back to me. I had to get an out. Only one thing to do.

Wind up, pitch – straight into his butt cheek. Again.

Ricky dropped his bat and started walking towards the mound.

"It slipped," I said as I started to laugh and back away at the same time.

"Next time I'm not stopping here," Ricky was grinning, "I mean it now." He walked back to the wall, picked up his bat and squared up. "You know where I can't get it, c'mon on. Try it, right up here," and he motioned to a spot in the air. He was always doing stuff like that. Even though he was just naturally better (and a bit bigger and faster) he encouraged me, gave me tips and pep talks and stuff. He was my best friend, and a good dude. "Bring it on, c'mon man." He was making little circular motions with the bat resting on his shoulder.

I stopped for a second, just slowing myself down. I really wanted to make this pitch. Exhale, look up, wind up and throw. Ricky didn't swing this time, and the ball bounced off the wall in the top outside corner of the box. Strike. I think Ricky let it go on purpose.

"See?"

"Ah, you're just happy I didn't hit you in the ass again."

"A little. Ok come on, for real now."

Pitching wasn't even the biggest issue, catching was. Being a catcher required special equipment that we couldn't afford. The only time we had it was at our league practices and games, and it was property of the park district. Even if we could afford it most of us didn't want to be a catcher. The gear was hot, you had to squat all the time, and there was a very low chance of making a diving catch or turning a double play or robbing a homer, which was all we wanted to do. Without the pads, glove, and facemask it was also pretty dangerous because while most of us had decent velocity, we all lacked consistent control, so there was a high likelihood of getting hit or having to block a throw in the dirt, and no cup meant that a curve attempt into the dirt in front of the plate was going to be a ball to the nuts more often than not.

So, we needed a way to not only play shorthanded, but without a catcher. The solution was pretty simple, all you need is a roll of duct tape (or spray-paint if you were up for a little casual vandalism) and a wall with a field opposite, just like the one behind Emerson Elementary.

According to the rules of Major League Baseball, the strike zone is essentially an imaginary rectangle the width of home plate, the top at your shoulders and the bottom at your knees that the ball has to go through for a called strike. So, against the wall you re-created this rectangle with paint or tape – the Hotbox. The plate was scratched into the ground away from the wall with a stick or rock or whatever. It was more of a visual cue for the batter than anything else.

Since we were all pretty close in age and size it wasn't that big of a deal if the box was a little high or low. Everyone had to use the same strike zone. Sometimes you had to deal with a high fastball that normally would be out of the zone for you but that's just how it works. The batter would stand next to the box on the wall, the pitcher would stand on the "mound" which was more like a trench we had all rubbed into the ground to brace our back leg against and then you had as many outfielders as you had people left. A pitch that hit inside the Hotbox was a strike (as was a swing and a miss), outside was a ball.

Scoring was based on distance, not baserunning. Caught on a fly anywhere was an out, on the ground was a hit. There was no infield or outfield, it was more like the lines on a soccer field. Up to the fence gate was a single, the blue garage across the alley that was at the halfway point of the field was a double, into the actual diamond that was on the other side was a triple and over the fence was a homer. You could play with just two people, but really the minimum was three, and four was great, you could have a shallow fielder and a deep fielder. Every man for himself, and you just rotated in so the pitcher was next to bat, deep outfield moved shallow, shallow moved to pitcher and so on.

"Ahhh, nope."

Next pitch was a bit lower than I wanted, and Ricky took a good swing, but my brother chased it down for out number two.

"Nice catch." I said as he tossed it back in.

"Ok, last out, give me your best shot, right here," Ricky was taking check swings in front of the box, kinda wagging the bat a bit.

"My best? OK, hit this."

I had been working on a split-finger fastball, and I wasn't sure exactly how well I had mastered it, but whatever. No time like the present to see how it worked. I threw, and it stared out ok but ended up coming out of my hand weird and bouncing off the wall about four feet to the right of Ricky's head.

"What was that..." Ricky laughed.

"Just a little something I've been working on. *Shut up!*" My brother was laughing loudly in the outfield.

"OK no more messing around. Here comes the old number one," I said to Ricky, who was wagging the bat at me again. I wanted to go low and in, and it felt good when I let it go.

Ricky didn't swing, and it just caught the bottom inside corner of the box for a strike. "Sneaking one in there huh? Ok, we'll see. I got one on, all I need is a hit."

"We'll see." I wanted the same location for the next pitch, but it went low for a ball.

"Boooooooo," my brother yelled from the outfield.

"Don't forget you have to pitch to me next butthole," I yelled back.

Next one I got the height right but not the location, and Ricky connected for a solid line drive, but I was able to take a quick step left and snag it for his last out.

"Ok so I'm at four and you guys are both at two, right?" Ricky said as I walked in to take my turn batting.

"Yeah, for now. We'll see if he can get it in the zone this time," I said, tilting my head towards my brother. He was younger than us and therefore at a disadvantage when it came to pitching, but we didn't give him too much of a hard time about it. I could count on getting at least one run by walks when he was pitching though.

Ricky picked up his glove and started walking out towards the outfield. My brother was already on the mound. I picked up the bat and started loosening up.

Ricky stopped in front of the mound and said something to my brother. I couldn't see or hear what was going on because his back was to me. Then my brother handed him the ball and trotted back to the outfield.

"Hey … hey what's the deal? He pitches to me."

"Lineup change. Is that a problem?" Ricky said smirking, tossing the ball up and catching it with one hand.

I was figuring I could at least get a run or two off my brother, in part because I could just stand there and let him deal with his control issues, but now I was going to have face the guy I just hit intentionally. Twice.

"You can't do that!"

"Sure I can. I'll pitch for both of you. He's cool with it," he said, pointing out at my brother, "That's fair. Sorta." He shrugged.

I did not agree, but there was nothing I could do about it. "Ok fine, but remember I never hit you anywhere important."

"Oh, I remember all right."

Because we were throwing a ball against a brick wall, a standard league ball wouldn't work because the batter would still have to shag pitches and that was what a lot of this was designed to avoid. Plus, it would ruin the ball pretty quickly, and those things weren't cheap. The best ball was one that was the same size and shape of a hardball but made of rubber. It had the seams molded onto it and everything, and they had them by the basketful at the toy store for like twenty-five cents each. All of the neighborhood kids had at least one, which was good because those things were always landing on the roof or over a house and gone somehow. Even if you kept it around eventually they would dry out and chunks would start breaking off. But they were the best.

Ricky was a shortstop, but that didn't mean he couldn't pitch a bit. "Gimme a couple warmups, stand back a sec," he said, motioning me off to the side with his glove hand. He took a few pitches, throwing harder each time. Every one was hitting right next to the box, right where I would be standing. "Ok ready."

"You sure you don't want a couple more? Those were pretty far inside."

"I'm good."

I stepped up to the box, bat gripped a little tighter than normal.

The bat of choice was aluminum. Even the lightest wooden bats were too heavy for some kids, and most of the league teams we played on all used aluminum bats so it's what we were used to. Besides, when you use an aluminum bat with a rubber baseball stuff is going to get lively and that's what we were after. There were no boring outfield turns, you had to keep on your toes because there was really no telling how far, how fast, or lots of times even which direction the ball was going to be coming off the bat in. It was great.

Of course, the first pitch Ricky threw was way inside, but I hopped back out of the way.

"You know you're supposed to be aiming for this box on the wall, right?"

"It slipped."

None of us had invented or painted the Hotboxes at Emerson. They were already there on the wall when we got there years ago like ancient cave paintings left by a previous generation for us to find, decipher and utilize. We may have run into these ancient elders once time. We got to the field one day and there were some older long haired dudes wearing concert shirts with jersey sleeves, jeans, and aviator sunglasses playing against the wall. They had a boom box and were listening to the Doors. They may possibly have been the original Painters of the Box, or maybe they found them there just as we did. They were all smoking, and it was hard to tell if they were potential friend or potential foe with those shades on, so we just gave it some space and didn't ask.

I guess that's who I thought was heading down the alley today when I first saw them. Four guys with long hair, black jeans, concert t-shirts and denim jackets. They came around the corner and were walking towards the school down the gravel alley that ran along the fence on the west side of the field. One guy had what looked to be those studded leather wristbands. Ricky and my brother had their backs to them, so they didn't see them. They didn't look familiar, but on second look I recognized the dude in the Ozzy shirt. It was James Barlow.

They weren't paying any attention to us. We were on the other side of the field anyway, so I wasn't super worried, I knew if we had to we could probably get away pretty easily, I guess depending on what they were up to, which right now was nothing but walking towards the end of the alley. There was kind of a gravel turn around for cars behind the rear wall of the school, but there was a footpath that lead you into the playground on the other side.

By now my brother and Ricky both saw the group, and we all watched them for a minute, but they weren't doing anything we could see, and they didn't seem to be interested in us, so we went back to the game. They were hanging out in the gravel turn-around talking to each other and smoking.

It was a big mistake to assume they weren't up to anything. I had my back to them because I was batting, but Ricky looked over and yelled *"Heads up!"* at me, as my brother started running in from the outfield. I turned around and saw two of them tossing what I initially thought were little tube smoke bombs over the fence.

Those tube smoke bombs are about the same size as m-80's, which is what they turned out to be. I'm not sure what the exact blast size of an m-80 is, but in my head it's the equivalent of like four firecrackers going off at once. Not a huge blast, but a good bang, and not something that was ok to hold in your hand when it went off.

The two m-80's blew, and then James tossed one more out there, but it was for sure not an m-80. It was bigger, and you could tell by the way it went off. First there was a flash, then a puff of smoke, then a BIG "boom." Had to be an M-1000 which was a quarter stick, that sucker was loud, and we were glad we weren't anywhere near the blast.

Ricky yelled, "What was that for? What the hell man, we weren't even doing anything to you."

James and his buddies were laughing and mocking what Ricky said, "What the hell maaaaaan, waaaaaa waaaa hahahaha."

Ricky was starting to lose his cool." You got a problem?" He yelled over at them. He took the bat out of my hands and started to walk towards them. "Let's go guys," he said to us, but we weren't as confident, or maybe not as angry as he was so we weren't so sure.

James casually lifted his shirt and uncoiled a bike chain he had looped through the belt loops of his pants.

"Ok, hey man, ok that's enough, there's four of them and James has a chain. Not now," I had Ricky's arm and was pulling him back, and my brother got in front of him, putting both hands on his chest.

We just picked up the rest of our stuff and left, with Ricky giving them the finger as we walked through the gap in the fence on the far side of the field. They were all laughing and whistling and jeering, waving goodbye as we made our exit. I could feel my ears getting hot, and I was sure my face was turning red and flushed. Those guys sucked, but now that the situation had diffused, I was curious about the firepower he had.

"Where is he getting that stuff? We know how much m-80's cost, and that last one had to be a quarter stick, those things are like five bucks a piece. I know he doesn't have a job. How can he afford to just toss those around?"

"I don't know, but I'm getting real tired of that dude's crap."

"Yeah me too, but there's more of them and if James has a chain who knows what the rest of them might be carrying. I don't think we should go back."

"I don't mean we do something right now, but I think it's time to put the you-know-what in his you-know where."

"What? What are you guys talking about?" My brother had not been let in on our stink bomb plan, primarily for secrecy reasons, but also because he had really bad luck when it came to fireworks mishaps, and we didn't want to add that risk to an already risky plan.

"Nothing, nothing for you to worry about. Hey, let's go to my yard and play running bases instead, ok? You can run first." Ricky treated my brother like his own. He seemed to be completely calmed down now too, which was a relief.

We walked back through the alley, and I paused for an extra second to look at the Barlow's garage before hopping the fence into Ricky's yard. I knew just the you-know-what that would go you-know-where, and I was going to get it first thing in the morning.

4

DEACON'S MAGIC SHOP

My parents were already gone when I got up the next morning, so I left a note on the table for my brother, "*Going to the mall, back soon,*" and got on my bike to go to Deacon's for the stink bomb. I was riding north down Grove Street towards Coolidge Park, lost in thoughts of nothing, enjoying cruising on my bike on a summer day. I wanted to ride down the hill in the park first, which was why I was headed up Grove, when a small red and white plastic State Farm football bounced off my back.

"Heads up, Peaches!"

I did not have a cool nickname. My nickname, "Peaches," originally was only a neighborhood thing. One of the younger kids couldn't say my name (Pete) but could say "peach" which was pretty close. Ricky modified it to Peaches, and the other kids just started calling me that too. I didn't mind too much because it was only around the block, not at school or baseball. At first.

We were at baseball practice, Ricky at shortstop and me in centerfield. I had tracked down a long fly ball and he was the cutoff man, waving his arms for the throw and yelling "Hit me, hit me!" and I guess I was taking a little longer than he wanted, because he yelled "Let's go Peaches, hit me!" Ricky swears it just popped out, so I wasn't that mad at him, but from that point on I was "Peaches" everywhere. I was a little irritated at first, but it grew on me, and I guess I just learned to accept it. Like Matty said later, "Hey man, peaches are delicious. Everybody loves 'em. Quit being a crybaby about it unless you want us to start calling you that instead." So, Peaches it was.

"Hey!" I stopped. There was a stocky kid with a backwards baseball hat standing in the front yard. A BMX bike was lying next to him on one side, and what looked like a five-gallon bucket full of small plastic footballs on the other. I waved and picked up the football. "Hey Matty! Nice throw."

The little plastic footballs from the insurance agency were awesome. Their office was on a corner, so they had two huge windows, and they had filled both windows about halfway up with these small red and white footballs that we had been eyeing for nearly two weeks on our way to and from school. They were left over from some promotion they had been running last fall, but now that it was summer they were probably tired of having boxes and boxes of the things laying around. I'm not sure who had decided to just walk in and ask for one, but once they opened the flood gates we all got our hands on at least a few. I think they got a little tired of us coming in there after a while, and honestly the novelty had kinda worn off for most of us as well, but either Matty was obsessed with them or wanted to see how far he could push it and apparently had been stopping in every day even though school was out and now he had to make a special trip.

I met Matty playing baseball, all the way back when we both started in t-ball. Now he was a catcher, and a good one. We were on the same team this year in our official league, playing for Olsen Foods, and had been on teams together off and on for years. He was also one of the most eloquent and accomplished cussers I had ever heard. Even though we didn't go to the same school it seemed like we always ended up together, and he lived close enough to Emerson that he was practically one of us neighborhood rats. We were tight.

"Going to Coolidge Park?" Matty knew my preferred routes.

"Yeah, gonna hit the hill quick and then I'm going to Deacon's."

"Cool. You should stop by the movie theater, they're giving out alien finger puppets, some promotional thing. They look like tan frogs, but I think you could fit an m-80 inside."

"Oh nice, I'll have to check them out. You got m-80's?"

"Nah. Well I mean I did, but my mom figured out they weren't smoke bombs like I told her, so she tossed my room and confiscated all my stuff, totally sucked. I still got some bottle rockets though, and I'm connecting with that dude Hansen for some firecrackers, but I have a hard time listening to him talk and talk and talk about explosion mechanics and attack vectors or whatever."

"Heh yeah, he does seem a little too into it, but he's got a *lot* of stuff this year. Anyway, if that don't work out let me know, I might be able to set you up with something."

"Cool man, thanks. Game today, see you later," he said pointing at me.

"Yup. See you later Matty," and I threw the football back at him, which he caught and put back in his bucket. Not wanting to miss out on free alien frog finger puppets I changed course and headed west towards the mall, planning to hit the park on my way back.

The mall was a good example of urban planning gone wrong. Years ago, the last few blocks of one of the main streets through town was permanently blocked off to traffic and redone with brick walkways and planters and fancy wrought iron streetlights. The concept was good – make it more like a town square, open-air shopping, design around people not cars, blah blah. Unfortunately, what happened was the businesses on the edges did well because there were well-travelled streets and some parking bordering the walkways, but due to the general lack of parking and easy accessibility the middle of the mall was dead. Soaped over windows, empty store fronts, the more "questionable" businesses like the record shop that had a huge Dark Side of the

Moon prism on the front and a large "for tobacco use only" section in the back were all that was there.

It's funny to think about all the planning that went into this people centric "we don't need cars here" destination and the one thing they didn't address was how people were supposed to get there and where they were supposed to leave their cars once they did. They ended up building an indoor mall on a corner of the dead zone a couple years ago and put a parking garage about three blocks away. Indoor malls were hot, I had been to the brand new one in the city with glass elevators and fountains and a food court so I understood the appeal. It was a strange fix though, like they wanted to use another mall to solve the problems of the first mall?

However, at the "good" end was an excellent movie theater, complete with the big marquee and its name in neon and light bulbs. I pulled up and got off my bike. There was no bike riding in the mall, against the rules. I usually didn't worry about that rule, it's just that now there were actually people here, a pretty good crowd in front of the theater. Normally you could just whizz right through unbothered.

I snagged a couple finger puppets. Matty was right on both counts, they did look like tan frogs, and you probably could fit an m-80 in one so win/win there and walked my bike west. Around the theater were a few restaurants and stores that seemed to be doing well; Kroch's & Brentano's books, Cunningham-Reiley sporting goods, Pompeii Pizza, and an Indian restaurant that had weird staying power. There were some knickknack/homemade jewelry/custom leather type places sprinkled in here and there rounding it all out. It's too bad, if they could have replicated this all the way down the mall it would have been really nice.

I got to the end of the street, past the Gap and Pier One that were like the demarcation lines of where business and traffic dropped off, took a left and then a quick right down a side street that ended in a completely pointless cul-de-sac.

In between a little neighborhood pharmacy that had a cut stone façade and a standard issue Chicago hot dog joint was Deacon's Magic Shop. It wasn't that big of a place, kind of nondescript from the outside, just one display window over which was a simple blue sign with gold letters spelling "Deacon's Magic" going all the way across. Bells on the door tinkled as you walked in, and there was a faint smell that was a combination of library, rubber chickens and something burnt.

Inside was beyond magic. I felt like they had mined my imagination for their inventory list. The layout was a lot like a pawn shop, with glass display cases around the perimeter, shelves and racks in the center, but it was all organized into categories in the different sections.

First thing you saw, right in front by the door, were the gags and joke items. Whoopee cushions, itching powder, fart sprays, cans with spring loaded snakes, hand buzzers, big rotating racks of that stuff. Stink bombs of varying sizes and potency we never had the nerve to set off indoors. Squirting lapel flowers. Squirting sunglasses. Little contraptions you could stick under a toilet seat that would squirt water up when someone sat down. A bin full of rubber chickens next to a bin full of rubber rats.

Past that stuff and heading towards the back were the clown supplies, all the way back into the corner -

wigs, noses, six-foot-long multicolor ties. Juggling pins, juggling rings, little tiny bikes, gigantic sombreros that you could fit a little dude in. Of course, special clown face paint. And shoes, but from what I understood they were more for display purposes and had to be special ordered in the correct size (really) once you chose a style.

But speaking of face paint, they had all of it, from cheapo Halloween stuff to professional theater quality. Fake mustaches of every color and size. Spirit gum. Grease paint. For those who weren't so skilled with face painting and disguise, around the entire perimeter, on two shelves near the ceiling, was nothing but masks of every kind – superheroes, monsters, presidents, rockstars, aliens.

All that stuff was awesome, and I'm sure it helped with overhead, but the magic gear was next level. It took up most of the display cases and shelves on the west side of the store. They had everything, and I do mean *everything*. Wands that turned into flowers. Wands that turned into rope. Wands that turned into silks. Wands that would squirt water (of course). Vanishing coin tricks, multiplying and disappearing coins, cups and balls, magic ring, magic rope, top hats, silks, all of it. There was a shelf of "50+ Magic Tricks – Fool Your Friends!" type kits, but we avoided those because we weren't beginners. They also had the big expensive elaborate illusions for stage magicians along the wall, like the separated lady, disappearing rabbit in a cage, levitating tables, and some of the other bigger prop stuff that pros used.

Card magic was its own section, and it was almost too much to comprehend because of the sheer variety.

Decks of cards from the size of a matchbook all the way up to the size of a poster. Every color and pattern, to no color or pattern, just blank cards. Weird little kits and packs of strings and wires and wax to levitate or spin cards. Marked decks of every make and design, including ones that were marked with special inks that you had to wear special sunglasses (sold separately) to see the markings on. Tapered decks to force cards. Cut and restored card tricks, appear in the envelope tricks, everything is the number seven. They had a whole shelf of decks that were just one card of every card.

But the best section of the store, for me at least, was the surveillance/private eye/secret agent gear. My fascination with espionage was deep. As soon as I was old enough, my mom got me a library card. We went to the library a lot, together at first but once I was old enough to ride my bike there I would go on my own, it was right next to Coolidge Park. Fiction wasn't really my thing back then and besides, my parents had bookcases full of books they had collected over the years, as students and then as teachers. If I was interested in literature or composition or the classics all I had to do was go into the living room and pick something out. What I loved at the library was the non-fiction and reference sections.

I don't know why I had wandered into the shelves with books about the FBI and Melvin Purvis and the CIA and spying on "the Soviets." It seemed so interesting, equal parts action and intelligence. There were stories about double agents and double crosses, microfilms hidden in hollowed out nickels and exchanged at dead drops in Central Park. Men in fedoras and trench coats, shoes with hollowed out heels that had a little mini kit of a knife and string and I forget what else that might be useful. I liked the gadgets and gizmos and sneaking around parts quite a lot. I also liked the "surviving on wits and knowledge" stories. Covert operatives in enemy territory making their way around undetected without much gear, blending in if they had to and slipping away into the forest. So cool.

For a long time, it was my career goal to be an agent of some kind. I assumed that when I was old enough to get a real job I would have learned so much and invented enough of my own gizmos that I could walk into the FBI and tell them "I'm ready to go, what do you want me to do first?" and they would be grateful I was there. I took it seriously, read as much as I could and tried to think of every scenario and then learn how to handle it.

I went through an outdoor survival phase, which was fine because the library had a pretty big section on just that. Dan Beard's *Camp Lore and Woodcraft* (what I think eventually became the official Boy Scout handbook) was amazing. The illustrations were all hand drawn diagrams and sketches and plans, and it was really easy to understand, and useful. You could find everything from snares for small game, how to make different types of shelters depending on the environment you found yourself in, how to make fire using whatever, how to tie every kind of knot in the universe. My dad took us camping – like backpacking in with what you need camping, not park the car and pitch a tent camping – and several tricks and tips came in handy out there.

My favorite subjects in these books were about tracking and trapping and staying undetected. I learned so many camouflage techniques. This led to the discovery of more military-focused handbooks and survival guides and *that* was where I discovered booby traps. The combination of all the wilderness trapping and snares I had learned with the opportunity to scale it up and try it on people was too much to resist.

I will say right here that I never wanted to seriously injure anyone. I had an appreciation for chaos for sure, but not on a large scale and never using lethal force. Tricks and pranks and just being a sneaky irritating little turd who managed to get away with minor destruction was about the extent of my "operations" and to be honest, a lot of it just didn't play out how the book said it would. This may have been discouraging for some kids but for me it was the opposite, I tried crazier and more elaborate stuff because I figured at some point the averages would be on my side and something would work, because most of the time it did not.

There was also a lot of needless complications. Taking apart a walkie talkie so you could put the microphone under something and wire it to be transmitting was a fun project, but I could have accomplished the same thing by just taping the "talk" button down and stashing the whole handset under a couch or behind some books. Making a hidden system of pulleys and clothespins and dental floss that would drop a little powder packet on someone's head was quite an operation, and the same thing could be accomplished with a good throw from the right position.

Once we started to get the hang of it, we booby trapped everything we could. I had all of kinds of tripwires and crap everywhere, so much so that usually the person setting it off was me. I was like a squirrel that hid nuts for the winter and then forgot where.

There was excellent selection of items at Deacon's for the amateur field agent. Sunglasses with little mirrors in the bottom corners of the lenses so you could see behind you. Hand-sized parabolic mics to hear conversations across the room. A whole rack of disappearing ink pens and papers and notebooks of various sorts. Pads of flash paper that would completely incinerate when ignited, to protect sensitive messages from falling into the wrong hands. Code books. Code rings. Disguises. Ordinary looking items that were hollowed out or had false bottoms that you could hide stuff in like books or soda cans. Mini binoculars. Mini monoculars. Periscopes and tubes with lenses for looking around corners or up into windows. Magnifying glasses. Fingerprint kits. Trip alarms. Fake "investigator" badges in little flip open wallets.

I could have hung out for a while; they were really cool to us and didn't care how long we spent in there. Honestly, we were probably some of their most regular customers, but I had a mission and needed to get back, so I chose the gnarliest stink bomb I could afford. According to the package, the "putrid smell would linger for days," which I felt was pretty much the message we wanted to send.

The delivery method was going to be the trick though. The Barlows had big picture windows in that shiny kitchen that looked out into the backyard, and they were always hanging out in there so we couldn't just chuck a rock and then the stink bomb – there was no way to get within range without being seen. That's OK though, we were confident we could figure out a way to both break the window and get the stink bomb in, using our favorite solution to problems - fireworks.

I took one last look at the magic decks to see if I had missed anything new and headed back home. I had a little time, so I wanted to try to find a smoke bomb in my stash that was close in size to the stink bomb for testing purposes before I had to meet up with Ricky.

5

WE HAVE FOUND THE ENEMY

There was a line that Deacon's Magic wouldn't cross or maybe couldn't cross, legally. Things like lockpick sets, universal keys, certain zoom lenses for cameras and of course all manner of "self-defense" gear like telescoping whip batons and handcuffs. All different types of miniature microphones that could be stuck under tables or chairs, some that went into the receivers of telephones, or in light fixtures. Security cameras, at least commercially available ones, were all of the closed-circuit system type, only seen in banks or at the police station. Portable video cameras were available, but they were so far out of our price range they didn't exist to us. None of this gear was stocked at Deacon's, but you could find it if you knew where to look.

We did know where to look. It was all in the back of martial arts magazines and comic books. Advertisements like "Hear Your Friends'

Conversations!" and warnings like "For Law Enforcement/Licensed Private Eye Only!" in the back of the latest Wolverine or Batman (depending on who you were into) let you know where to get the good stuff. We would send off $1.75 for our catalogs from J&J Military and Police Surveillance Supply Services Company Limited, and then anxiously check the mail every day for four-to-six weeks until it arrived. In a plain manila envelope would be a "catalog" that was stapled together photocopied black and white complete weirdness.

Mr. Barlow, James Barlow's dad, would most definitely have been in on stuff like this if he had seen it. For all we knew he was. While he shared the same commitment as his son to taking weird and unsafe and combining them into a lifestyle, he was much more creative and much less violent about it.

In the late 70s there was a "pet rock" craze. It was a gag thing, but they sold an insane amount of what was just a rock, but it came with all kinds of accessories and instructions for care and feeding and what not. Mr. Barlow was convinced that he was going to be the next millionaire by finding the next pet rock, and he was thoughtfully working his way through various objects until he found the correct one. His current object was a stick.

I don't know if this was a side business or his main thing or what. He was another one that no one really knew what he did for a living, but they didn't seem to be doing too bad so whatever it was paid pretty well. What we did know was that he had several thousand "Pet Sticks" in his garage, like pallets stacked high with boxes full of them. They didn't even park cars in there because there was no room for them.

We liked him ok enough though. When we did see him, he was always giving us a Pet Stick or asking what we thought about his next idea for inanimate pets. Also, he loved the gag section at Deacons, and you could bet if he shook your hand you were going to get zapped by a hand buzzer. We learned quickly to never smell any flowers he offered because it would end up with a face full of water. We could relate to him because he seemed like us sorta, only older and better financed.

A few years later the first editions of *The Anarchists Cookbook* started getting passed around bulletin boards and I suspected that the people who put out these catalogs were heavily involved in some portions of its creation, and I wouldn't have been surprised if Mr. Barlow was involved somehow as well.

Checking out that stuff was one thing, but ordering it was not something we were going to do, for a couple good reasons. For one, most of these order forms required a photocopy of your PI license or law enforcement ID, which none of us had and didn't think that we could forge, although in hindsight we totally could have. I don't think the barrier was as high as we envisioned.

The other reason, the biggest reason really, was price. The professional stuff in these catalogs looked to be the same stuff law enforcement used and was top of the line, and we did not have that kind of money. But all our dads had workshops and tools either in the basement or the garage, and we just figured if we couldn't get what we needed from Deacon's or we couldn't afford it, we could come up with something ourselves. That's what our dad's did in their workshops, so we assumed we could too.

Coming up with ideas for stuff wasn't the hard part. Making it work was the hard part, and while we had a lot of ideas, we did not have a lot of success. There was a lot of over engineering. If a simple switch couldn't be activated with a series of pulleys and string, the obvious solution was more pulleys and more string. There was also the risk of injury from both unsuccessful and successful testing.

My friend Rob, who lived down the block, was working on a silent explosive delivery system using his BB gun. He was actually on to something here; I think most of the big theme parks switched over to a similar concept using compressed air to launch their fireworks for big shows years later. After numerous prototypes he had ended up with a firecracker taped to a length of piano wire, with tape wrapped around the other end so it would be snug and sealed in the barrel of the rifle, and it actually worked. It was primitive, but functional. There was an equal chance it would not go off at all, it would go off in the barrel, or it would fire and go in the direction you were aiming. It was option two that happened with the most frequency until the final failed shot with a larger firecracker, a Black Cat Plus, that ended up blowing the seals out of the gun so it would no longer hold pressure.

Aside from demolition and surveillance objectives, some of us were developing other useful inventions. My brother was prototyping a piece that would let you jump into your pants, and then jump again and your pants would be pulled up, hands free. I believe speed was the objective here, but I could also see my brother imagining a world where everything was either jumped into or on and off of and this was the logical start of things.

I wasn't involved in the creation of the final prototype, but I was there for the final test, which involved jumping off the kitchen counter into the pants device, and then jumping up again for the mechanism to pull the pants up.

As we were sitting in the emergency room waiting room, after explaining in detail the intricacies of the system and stages of operation while my brother was holding a rag onto the gash in his head that would require six stitches to close, my mom said, "What is wrong with just pulling your pants up like everyone else?" my brother said, "Well, this is easier."

It's funny, we spent so much time researching and studying and prototyping and testing. An embarrassing amount of time. But there was one fundamental problem that we managed to skirt for my entire secret agent career, and it was this: who exactly were we supposed to be spying on? We left notes for each other in dead drops, coded notes in fact, that said things like "meet me in the park at 3:00" or "stay ready" but we were not exchanging stolen microfilms or plans. We had no purpose.

The only time we actually got into it for real was when we noticed that the people who lived between the Keltons and the Swensons started parking their cars in the street instead of the garage suddenly. No one parked on the street, especially overnight. Naturally we assumed they were fabricating something illicit in there or storing some contraband of some kind. They had to be up to something, we reasoned, why else would they park the car on the street, directly in front of their house? In broad daylight, too.

When we found out that the reason the garage was cleared out was because some racoons had gotten in and were making a mess of things, we switched the focus of our operations to the racoons. The raccoons seemed to congregate in a yard across the alley behind Rickys house, so we set up a command post in his garage.

I know a lot of people think racoons are cute smart little guys who are like big harmless squirrels. Maybe they've only seen them in zoos or on TV, or they're different out in the woods or something, because the urban racoons we were familiar with were not cute or small in any way. They were probably on average about 20-25 pounds each, and that's average. We had seen some probably pushing 35 pounds for sure. I had seen them standing with their back feet on the ground and front feet at the top of the three-foot chain-link fence in my backyard. They are closer to small bears than big squirrels, and in our experience had the same temperament. Also, they travelled in groups, officially called a "gaze" according to the book I checked out from the library, but I think "gang" would be a better description.

Racoons were also known to carry rabies, and we had been warned often not to fool around with them unless we wanted to get a trip to the hospital that included a series of 10 shots in the stomach if one of them bit us. I'm not sure if the round of shots in the stomach was true or urban legend, but it was enough of a deterrent to keep us from tangling with them up close if we could avoid it.

Through the course of Operation Really Pointless, we also placed under surveillance the "suspicious" person who lived across the alley, but suspicious was probably a little generous. I don't think he invited the raccoons into his yard, and we didn't actually see him interact with them in any way, so we were unable to establish a link between this individual and the racoons. Really the dude just spent a lot of time in his back yard and on the back porch, sometimes talking on the phone that he had run out there through the kitchen window. Honestly, *we* were the most suspicious people in the neighborhood.

The raccoons were acting on their own, and they were definitely up to something. Maybe. It was hard to tell what was suspicious and what was regular raccoon behavior, and they weren't always so easy to find unless it was the night before garbage day. But the facts were they did get into the neighbor's garage and did cause damage in there, and across the alley from Ricky's felt a little too close, so we knew some kind of action needed to be taken. We just weren't sure what.

Further complicating things, my brother had started to like the raccoons the more time he spent observing them. He always had a big heart when it came to animals, and I guess he just appreciated their resourcefulness. The little ones were kinda cute I guess, but the rest of us would prefer them be cute somewhere a little further away from where we hung out.

We decided to solve the problem with our new favorite booby trap. Most of our fireworks activity happened in the alley, and the raccoons gave us a wide berth when we were out there because they didn't like the explosions, so we knew they had a weak point and decided to exploit it.

For three nights in a row, we set up the firecracker

and birthday candle trick in back of Ricky's garage near the garbage cans. It was hard to tell if it was working though. They were going off for sure, but the racoons, while maybe a little jumpier, kept coming back. We were getting a little frustrated but were undeterred. The three of us were filing through the gate to set the trap for the evening:

"You can't lie to the FBI it's against the law."

"No way. Really? What if I didn't know? Like, do they tell you that first?"

"I don't think they have to."

"I wonder what other people you can't lie to."

"Like judges?"

"No I mean like someone else I wouldn't know about. Like the coast guard."

"Have you been lying to the coast guard?"

"I don't think so, but now I'm not as sure as I used to be. O hey - I got something extra for them tonight," Ricky was saying to me and my brother as we headed out into the alley.

It was still daylight, but the sky was getting pale as the sun set. The alley was empty, no other kids or raccoons or anything back there. We reached the usual spot and Ricky pulled a small silver tube-shaped firework out of his pocket. It was a Silver Server. I don't know what the special ingredient in them was, but the difference between a Silver Server and an m-80 was flash. An m-80 would go off with a boom, but a Silver Server was a boom and bright flash, like the professional cameras the used for school pictures. I thought it was a pretty good idea. My brother did not.

"Hey c'mon now, that's too far. I don't like any of this in the first place, but you can't use one of those on them!" My brother had been struggling with all of this. He had started to consider the raccoons his friends, even named one of them "Bandit," although we didn't know how he could tell them apart, so they were pretty much all named "Bandit" I guess.

"Relax man, it's just a little more bang and flash, you know these things aren't that big."

"Yeah but they haven't done anything to us! They're just trying to survive, and you guys have to go and mess around with them, can't we just leave them alone? Why do you care if they are getting in the garbage, it's *garbage* no one wants it anyway."

"I'm fine with them surviving, I just want them to do it somewhere else. If they get into my garage my dad is going to make *me* clean it out. Have you seen all the stuff in there? We could get the Mustang taken out, that's no good. I'm sorry dude but we gotta do this."

Seeing Ricky was unmoved he turned to me, "Please? Can't we try putting some cans on a string or something else to scare them away?"

Maybe we could have tried something like that, but I felt like we had already come this far with the firecrackers, and they didn't seem to be a deterrent, I couldn't see how some cans on a string would be any more effective. Besides, I liked setting off stuff using our little birthday candle trick, it was fun, and we were getting pretty good at it.

"Sorry man. This has gone on long enough, no other way. Besides, it's not like we're hurting them, we're sending a message. Like when a pitcher comes up and in to get you off the plate, that's all. We aren't going to hurt them, just give 'em a good brush-off."

I truly believed that when I said it. Thing is, the days

start to kinda run together once you're out of school in the summer, and I didn't realize it was Wednesday night. Tomorrow was Thursday, which was garbage pick-up day. The cans were full tonight, like every Wednesday night.

I'd like to think it wasn't our carelessness that led to what happened next. My brother had an unfortunate track record of being associated with fireworks mishaps, but since he was trying to stop us, in retrospect we really have no one to blame but ourselves.

By design we weren't there when it went off, but we were in the vicinity and heard the blast and then what turned out to be a raccoon screaming, and we got back there in time to see them hauling down toward the other end of the alley. There was a toppled garbage can, and some garbage was laying out in the alley.

"Oh man, did that go off *on* them?"

Ricky looked grim, "I think it did."

They must have been back there starting in on the usual Wednesday night feast when the Silver Server went off, and it was a double whammy for them. I can't imagine what it must have sounded like from inside that garbage can, and the flash must have been like lightning.

I still felt pretty bad about that. It did seem like it was effective though. We had not seen the raccoons around our end of the block too much, and when we did, they took off pretty quickly. I felt bad about that, too. I guess we never really thought that they would understand it was us who was setting off the fireworks, and I didn't like knowing that we were now what they feared and hated. Plus, my brother had gotten pretty mad at us, and I didn't think he was wrong to be either. We hadn't thought through all the different ways our plan *could* end, just the way we *wanted* it to end.

I was thinking about it as I rode my bike to Hillgrove with Ricky. I guess sometimes you come across a situation that you should stay out of, because there are some things you just shouldn't mess with, no matter how simple or harmless it looks from first glance. The problem I had with this lesson was that lots of times we couldn't differentiate "ok to mess with" from "not ok to mess with" until after we had messed with something, and it was too late to do anything about it if we were wrong.

6
AIN'T NO EASY OUTS

We were sitting on the bench in the dugout. The game hadn't started yet. Ricky was the expert on girls since he had a girlfriend, so he was instructing us on how to be "cool with the ladies." Most of us did not have girlfriends in the romantic sense. We all had girls we were friends with, and our buddies' sisters and stuff, but we hadn't quite crossed the gap into dating relations yet. It was still interesting though, and most of us were paying attention and filing away the advice for later use. "You can't curse too much. Like, there's a line - a little is OK, maybe even expected, but you can't go too far."

Matty needed clarification though, "What's too far?"

"I would say once you get into the f-word and above you're in dangerous territory."

"That doesn't really help. So I can still use…." Matty went on in an extensive and profane list of the words he considered to be less offensive than the "f" word.

"What? No. No …what's wrong with you?" Ricky

was waving his hands and shaking his head. "No dude, you can't say any of that. Jeeze"

"Matty, think of it this way," I said," if you can't say it in a PG movie then you can't say it to a girl."

"How am I supposed to … you mean I can't…." Matty was genuinely confused. "I don't understand this stuff at all." Most of the dugout felt the same.

The batting orders were exchanged, pitcher took his last warmups, and it was time to play. We were playing Gilcrest Hardware today and were the visitors, so we were batting first. Their second baseman was chanting "Easy out…. easy out…easy out…." at our leadoff hitter Robbie. He was a good kid, plenty fast, but he was also one of the younger guys on the team and not a consistent hitter. Coach Wilson was very cool about making sure everyone got a chance at different spots, and today he was giving Robbie the shot at leadoff.

"Jeeze man, shut that dude up already," Ricky was not appreciating the infield chatter. He put one hand to the side of his mouth and yelled, *"Hey c'mon Robbie let's get at one!"* towards the plate, and then put on a helmet and headed out to the on-deck circle.

I felt the same way, about that one in particular. For the past couple years, I had struggled with batting. I never had problems hitting playing Hotbox or when we were playing neighborhood pickup games, but once it was a real game, I don't know why but it froze me up. My confidence drained. That's probably why I didn't play full games. I was a liability on offense.

I wasn't the biggest or fastest kid on the team, but I wasn't the smallest or slowest either. Mechanically my swing was good, but for whatever reason I just couldn't put it all together in the batter's box during an actual league game. A lot of kids had the same problem. Even though it was just little league, maybe it was the uniforms or the umpire or whatever, but the pressure was real. The other teams knew it too. They used to call "Easy out" at me.

Not this year though. I don't know if I had grown a bit and that had improved my confidence, or if it was because I knew it was my last year and I just didn't feel the pressure as much anymore, or maybe both, but I felt like I could hit anyone who was pitching. Once I had to run laps in practice because I "watched it go for too long," when my coach was pitching during batting practice. He wasn't wrong, but he was also a little mad that I crushed his "unhittable" split-finger fastball too.

Eventually my coaches started throwing all kinds of weird crap at me in practice out of either frustration or curiosity because I could connect on just about anything. Not saying it was always a double or a homer, but if you needed contact, I was your guy. I turned it around so well I was hitting just under .310 for the season and made the All-Star team for the first time ever. No one said "Easy out" anymore when I got up to bat, but I remembered how it felt.

Today we were playing at Hillgrove Commons. It's a big park that had two diamonds, and we were playing on the one facing a steep embankment that led up to the "L" tracks. It was the best (and only) nearby hill for sledding in the winter, and a natural backstop for the outfield in the summer.

Robbie struck out, Ricky got a walk and I headed towards the batter's box. I looked down to our third base coach for the sign. It was "take" which means "don't swing" in baseball. Not an uncommon call for the first pitch, especially early in the game. You want to try to get the starting pitcher to throw a lot, get his pitch count up and wear him out so he doesn't have his best stuff as soon as possible.

I stepped into the batter's box, squared myself tapping the outside edge of the plate with the bat and got into the hitter's stance. The first baseman was tapping his glove against his thigh, leaning on one leg.

From behind me I could see the catcher's glove way out to the right side of the plate, like so far out it was in my field of vision. Say what? Trying to get me to chase an outside pitch was fine, but this was like two feet off the plate. Weird, but OK I guess. Maybe they knew I could hit and were just trying to be careful? There was the regular infield chatter, nothing out of line. It was a little off.

Four pitches, all outside by a mile, and I was on first, Ricky advancing to second, one out. Aaron was up, another one of the younger guys, also not a great hitter yet. Second base had his hand in his glove and was chanting "easy out…. easy out…. easy out.." and swaying back and forth, not too concerned about Ricky or me either. There was a lot of chatter coming from the infield, all directed at Aaron.

First pitch was a heater right down the middle. "Strike one!" from the ump behind the plate. "See? Easy out…. easy out…" from the second baseman. Laughter and jeering from the infield. And then I happened to look over at the first baseman and he smirked. Just a bit of a lip curl and narrowing of the eyes. It felt like something was up, but I wasn't sure what.

I was friends with, or at least friendly with, a lot of kids who were on other teams and sometimes we'd give each other a little business, but it was never mean or personal. Hell, me and Ricky would give each other and all of the other kids in the neighborhood crap all the time, and they gave it back. I didn't know these two kids, and this was the first game of the year against Gilcrest Hardware so I couldn't really say from experience if they were just saying stuff to say stuff or if there was a deeper meaning to what was going on, but something felt weird. Why did I get walked like that?

Three more pitches and Aaron was out, followed shortly by Eric J., who also got the "easy out, hey battabattabatta" treatment, stranding me and Ricky out there. We jogged back to the dugout to trade our batting helmets for gloves and chatted as we jogged back out onto the field.

"That was weird, right?"

"Yeah. I think he pitched around me, he acted like he was having trouble with control and was all over the place, but he put it right in the zone for Aaron."

"Eric too."

The conversation ended as he split off to play shortstop and I headed for center field.

They went three up and three down, so we were back up in the top of the second, score still nothing to nothing.

Johnny Mac, my old t-ball teammate and a solid hitter, was leading off this inning, and he got four balls in the dirt. Standard infield talk, not even really directed at John.

The next few batters were probably the weakest part of the lineup until we got to Matty, and all three of them got the trash talking business from the infield AND outfield, as well as some well-located fastballs. They were practically laughing at our guys.

Maybe if they would have trash talked everyone we might not have caught on, or at least maybe wouldn't have caught on until it was too late, but the lack of crap me, Ricky, Matty and Johnny got compared to the massive amount of crap they were giving the younger guys stood out. I was leaning over the fence next to Ricky in the dugout and said "What's wrong with these guys? They aren't saying all that stuff to us. It's like they're picking on the grommets only." We affectionately called the rookies and second year kids "grommets."

Ricky turned to me, "Hey … hey I think they are just intentionally walking anyone who they think can hit and then taunting and fanning the grommets. They're playing head games man! They know we got more grommets than vets, I bet their coach is in on it too. He probably came up with it, that's not cool at all. Hey coach! Coach Wilson! LT!"

Ricky told Coach what he thought was happening. Coach Wilson looked down at his clipboard and was nodding, but we had to hustle out on field for the bottom of the inning so couldn't stay and talk.

They got a little bit going this inning, but Ricky turned a double play with a cleanly fielded grounder, and we were back in the dugout. While we were going in we saw Coach Wilson walk over and talk to their coach, then head back to us.

"You tell him to cut it out, Coach?" Ricky asked.

"Ah, sorta. He's playing dumb, says his pitcher is just like that, and the talk is just how his guys are, nothing out of line from his perspective, of course, but at least now he knows we know what's going on. Maybe," he said, looking bemused, "Technically it's not against the rules, but I agree with you guys, if that's what they're doing it's not right. I can't really do much officially," he said," I told him to give kids a chance, remember we are setting an example, sportsmanship and all that, but...." he just shrugged.

"So they can get away with it? We're just going to let them keep doing it?" Ricky was pleading with Coach Wilson, but I knew if there was something he could do he would have done it.

"Ricky, I know, but you gotta understand I don't have a lot I can do here. I can say something to the ump, but I don't know if he can do anything about it right now outside of a warning."

"What about us?"

"What do you mean? You want to try talking to the ump? I guess it could work, he looks closer to your age, maybe he can relate to you better."

"What? No, I don't want to talk to the ump. I meant if you can't do anything, let us handle it."

"Uhh yeah, I'm not so sure I like the sound of that. Remember, you're setting an example for these younger guys too. We have to play the right way even if other teams aren't."

"I know, but look," Ricky argued," they are counting on keeping us older guys out of scoring position, and the rookies have to strike out. All we need to do is mess that up a bit and it all falls apart. Just give us the green light every time we're up, we can do it without breaking any rules or anything. Please."

"No fighting. Promise. And if you do you will never play another inning on this team." Coach Wilson was giving Ricky a hard look. They knew each other pretty well but this was a big thing to ask. Ricky was really good, but he also didn't like getting messed with when he was playing and had been suspended for a couple games last year because he charged the mound after a pitcher came inside twice, after getting a warning.

"Hey, that was different. I promise, no fighting."

"OK. We'll try it, but keep it clean or you're getting benched, I mean it."

"Deal! Hey – guys! Listen up, c'mere, listen…."

We huddled up, and Ricky laid out what was going on. The plan, really more of a sketch in the dugout dirt, was to try to do whatever we could to push runners in to score. That meant that the younger guys were going to have to try to get on, and those of us that were getting pitched around were going to have to try to maximize both our plate and on-base chances.

"It's like pepper, just make contact even if it's outside the zone. We don't want them feeling safe about any pitch." Pepper was a batting practice game where you would stand against the fence with a bat and try to make contact with whatever got thrown at you, not letting anything get past, like a soccer goalie.

The easiest thing the grommets could do was crowd the plate. We told them to get up on it, "When the ump gives you a warning you'll know you're close enough," Matty the catcher told them. We did not tell them that the desired outcome of them doing this was to be hit by a pitch, but I think it was understood.

The other thing we told them was to swing or bunt if it looked like the pitch was going to be in the zone. Do anything but stand there for the entire at-bat. For the rest of the dugout that was not batting, make some noise, try to negate the taunting. There was a risk this would escalate it, but it felt good hearing people cheer for you anyway so psychologically we felt it was a net gain.

For us older guys, the goal was third base. Whatever we had to do but get to third base. Coach Wilson already had been smart with the lineup and made sure there weren't too many grommets batting in a row, so we felt like if we could at least get a guy on third with one out we could get him in. For all of us, vets and grommets, once you got on it was anything goes, just get to the next base.

Top of the order again and here we go. Robbie was up first, then Ricky, then me. We had a little hitters meeting before those two headed out.

"Ok Robbie, here's what I want you to do," Ricky instructed. "Crowd that plate, take that side away from him, that should get you ball one. He's going to adjust, so next pitch will be more of a location thing, hold up on that one. The pitch you want is the third pitch, ok? Swing at the third pitch."

Robbie nodded, we both patted him on the back, and he headed up to bat.

I looked at Ricky, "You serious?"

"It doesn't matter, he's throwing the same pitch to him every time, pretty much same spot too. But the first step to getting a hit...." he pointed at me.

"Is believing you can get a hit," I finished.

"Johnny Bench, man."

"Yup."

Robbie stepped in and they started right in on him.

"Easy out....easy out.....no swing...."

Robbie was right up on the plate, doing as he was told. Ricky was in the on-deck circle, so Robbie could see him, and he gave Robbie the "swing away" sign the coaches use, and clapped his hands, "Let's go Robbie! You got this guy."

Robbie did not have this guy. He didn't chicken out though, and he did what Ricky told him, taking a good swing at the third pitch before getting struck out looking at a fastball that was low but in the zone.

I high-fived him and tapped the back of his helmet as I headed out to the on-deck circle, "You did great man, just keep doing that, it's going to get to them." Everyone else in the dugout was congratulating him and patting him on the back like he got a hit.

Ricky was up. He made a big show of working his back foot into the dirt, squaring up into the batter's box, all that, but he was staring down the pitcher the entire time. Never broke eye contact from the moment he walked up there. He also crowded the plate.

Three outside pitches and one in the dirt later and Ricky was on first. He had stared down the pitcher the entire way and was still staring at him from first base. I knew he wasn't that mad, just trying to unnerve the guy a little.

I walked up to the plate and squared myself, went through the usual routine even though I was pretty sure they were going to walk me again. I don't know why I got so upset at that moment, but I did. *Why not just play it right, why are they making our guys feel bad?* I had had enough of it. I tried to keep it cool, stepped out of the box, picked up a little infield dirt and wiped it between my hands while looking down for the sign from my third base coach. It didn't matter what sign he gave me; I already knew what I was going to do.

Back foot in the batter's box, tapped the bat to the

opposite corner of the plate and squared up. Looked over at the first baseman and he was leaning on one leg with his mitt on his hip, smirking. I looked back at the pitcher, and he was getting ready for the windup. I could see the catcher in my peripheral vison, he was still crouched down but had his arm extended above his shoulders and way out to the right of the plate. They were walking me. Again.

Windup and pitch, and it was of course way outside, ball one. I relaxed my stance, rolled my eyes, didn't step out or go through any pre-hit routine like I normally do. I wanted them to relax and think I was going along for the ride. I stood there straight up for the next throw, didn't even bend my knees. This pitch was more of a hard toss to the catcher, about two feet off the plate. The ump didn't even get all the way down into position this time. Ball two.

For no real reason I had chosen the third pitch to be the one, maybe Ricky put it into my head earlier. I kept it cool, stepped out of the box while the catcher tossed it back to the pitcher, and then he went back behind the plate with his glove hand all the way out to the right, waiting for ball three.

Ball three was not what I had in mind. The pitcher wound up and threw, high and way outside of course, and bit harder than what I guessed it would be. Because I played Hotbox with my brother pitching, I had a much larger contact zone. This was no big deal for me, but no way would they be ready for it.

I had to step in and over the plate to swing, and the path of the bat never dropped, it was like a dead-level shoulder high swing, maybe slightly up. I'm not sure because I wasn't totally looking at it, I was also looking at the first baseman and imagining the ball lining off my bat directly at him. I didn't want to hurt him or anything, I guess I just thought he was already going to be surprised by me hitting it, so he would be *really* surprised by the ball coming right at him, and that was an amusing scene to envision. I had managed to space out mid-swing thinking about how funny that would look.

There is a sound a baseball makes when it's hit. If you've played for any length of time, or even watched enough games, eventually you can tell just by the sound how well the ball was hit. With wooden bats, there's a "pop" that's got a ring to it. There's a reason home runs are called "dingers," you can tell by the sound. There's a whole spectrum of pops and cracks though; fly outs and grounders just sound different, but that long hard fly ball sounds like nothing else. Aluminum bats have a different sound than wood, they go ding, but there's also a higher pitch metallic "ping" to it.

I don't know what I thought was going to happen. I didn't expect solid contact. Like *real* solid, and I heard the unmistakable ping. I swung late so it was actually headed towards the first base side. Oh man, I really didn't think this through.

But it wasn't a line drive headshot. It was a beautifully arcing deep fly ball high over the first basemen's head, straight down the first base line, staying fair. It went so far the right fielder had to turn around and run after it.

I was so surprised I just stood there watching it fly. I knew I was going to hit it, but I didn't think it would be like that. I was expecting a grounder. I had smashed it, like *really* smashed it. Blasted one. It was kinda quiet for a second. I think everyone was also surprised and also watching it sail and then Ricky, who was now leaving first since it was clear he wouldn't have to tag up said, "Whoa Peaches – *run!*" and took off. The whole dugout just started yelling "Go Peaches!"

I dropped the bat and ran, head down and chugging for first as hard as I could, which must have been funny to watch because that shot was a clear double. First base coach was just windmilling his arm "Go two, go two, go two!" I never even slowed down, just made the turn and headed for second.

Halfway to second I looked over at my third base coach and he had both palms up like he was lifting a plate and then held his hand up in the "stop" sign. Stand up double. Ricky on third. One out. Our dugout was going wild. I was strangely calm as I stopped and stood there on second base. Runners on second and third, one out. Their coach headed out to the mound, joined by the catcher and the rest of the infield.

Ricky was standing on third with his arms folded in deep discussion with Coach Mike, the third base coach. Aaron was up next. Second year kid, he could hit but was inconsistent. The meeting on the mound broke up, everyone trotted back to their positions. Aaron stepped in and the infield started up with the "easy outs" and "swing battabattabatta…"

I could hear them because I was out there in the infield, but I don't know if it made it to Aaron at the plate, because now our dugout was loud to the point of rowdy. A couple guys were banging the aluminum bats on the top of the dugout fence, and they were chanting "Aaron, Aaron, Aaron."

The pitcher got into the stretch since there were runners on. Our dugout stopped with the "Aaron," and started what I guess you could call a "vocal wave" – they were just going "oh" but started out quiet and got louder and louder as the pitcher went into the windup:

"oooooooooooOOOOOOOOOOOOOOOOOOO HHHHHHHHHHHHHHHH!"

I don't know which one of those grommets thought of it, but it was brilliant. And effective. First pitch was in the dirt, and the catcher had to block it with his body, but he was able to keep it in front of him. I looked over at third and Ricky was looking back at me, nodding. And grinning.

The catcher threw the ball back to the pitcher, and our dugout started up again:

"oooooooooooOOOOOOOOOOOOOOOOOOO HHHHHHHHHHHHHHHH!"

This time it went into the dirt and bounced to the right of the catcher, going behind him. Ricky took off for home and I took off for third. The catcher couldn't see where the ball was, flipped off his mask, turned around looking everywhere, located it, ran back and picked it up just as Ricky crossed home standing up and I made it to third. No throw. Our dugout was practically foaming at this point.

I guess we all figured third pitch was as good as any to take a shot, and that's what Aaron did, but he missed for a strike. Next one he made contact with but grounded to the shortstop. I held my base, so the only play was the force at first, which they made. Two outs, me still on third.

Eric J. was up next, and the dugout was now keeping a steady beat with whatever they could find to hit against something. Some kids were just clapping, and it was loud. Eric stepped into the batter's box. He was a lefty so he was on the first base side of the plate, and he was right on top of it.

First pitch was so far off the plate it went behind his back, which is scary for a batter, but he held his ground. It got Coach Wilson up yelling at the ump "What is that?" The ump motioned him back into the dugout and got back into position. Next one hit Eric in the thigh. He could have moved but didn't, just took the shot and then jogged down to first. Now our coach was out there again, and the ump called the other team's coach out and they had a brief discussion in front of the third base dugout before they broke up, with their coach going to the mound to talk to his pitcher. Coach Wilson came walking back to us looking sour.

"Watch your heads," was all he said.

Johnny was up next, and he was all business right now. The pitcher was too, but he did not look as sure of himself as he did a couple innings ago. I know he got a warning from both his coach and the ump, so he had to be careful.

I did not have to be careful, and I wasn't. I took a huge lead off third, which put the third baseman in a weird spot. I don't think they had changed their strategy of pitching around hitters, but my hit off an intentional walk gave them something to think about. The idea that Johnny would be going after any pitch he thought he could connect with added an element of unpredictability that the third baseman was now grappling with. Hold me on the bag or get in position for a hit?

The easy counter to this for them was a pitchout, which they tried but I was back in time to beat the throw from the catcher. Ball one.

Ball two was in the dirt, ball three was so far outside it hit the backstop. I took a couple extra steps towards the plate, but the ball took a good bounce and came back to the catcher too fast, so I just held up.

I didn't have the right angle from third to see the exact position, but I think he wanted ball four to be high and outside, but he wasn't outside quite enough and Johnny got around on it, sending it deep down the right side of the field but it hooked foul. Strike one.

What happened next was the pitcher overcompensated for being outside with the last pitch and wanted to go inside but went too far inside and almost took off Johnny's head. He hit the dirt but popped up quick, and our coach ran over to keep him from charging the mound. The ump tossed the pitcher right there. I was on third base still, so I was right in front of their dugout, so for sure they all saw me laughing and clapping the whole time the pitcher was walking back to the dugout. He had to walk right past me to get to the bench, and when he got close I could see his face.

I stopped clapping.

He looked shook up and hurt – and angry, and he was looking right at me like I was the one who caused it. I could see he was struggling, like he was trying not to cry in front of everyone. I'm guessing he'd never been thrown out before, and that combined with the idiotic strategy his coach pushed him into was a bit more than he could handle because he speed-walked past me into the dugout and put a towel over his face as soon as he got to the bench. I could see his shoulders heaving.

I felt … confused. They were in the wrong. Yes, technically what his coach was doing was not against the rules, but it was still crappy. We countered his mean-spirited strategy with a better one and it worked, but now this kid was paying the price and I guess I felt bad about that, but I didn't understand why. Out in the neighborhood kids cried, usually from injury, but sometimes frustration or anger or sadness. It was a tough day for us all when we found the kitten Pasha the Coyote got to first. Hell, I had made my brother cry plenty of times just doing sibling stuff, and he had gotten me too.

It wasn't even personal, at least it hadn't started out personal, at least I didn't think it had, but now that I saw this dude it became personal and not in a good way. We were the bad guys in his story. I was the bad guy. I should have been fine with that because we did the right thing, at least I thought so. But at the same time, I understood that he thought *he* was doing the right thing and we were on the wrong side of it.

Eventually I decided that third base wasn't a great spot to have an identity crisis so I pushed it aside and got back to the game at hand. I was interested to see if they were going to keep trying the same strategy now that it was pretty obvious we had figured out what they were doing and had come up with a successful counter.

Their new pitcher finished his warmup throws, catcher practiced a throw to second, the ump looked over at our dugout and motioned to the next batter, "Play ball," and we were back at it. No games this time, just standard infield chatter ,"Two outs, take any play." It seemed like they quieted down on the more direct taunting. The grommet batting swung on a decent fastball, connected, but didn't beat the throw to first and that was the end of the inning.

The rest of the game was drama free, but our dugout was still rowdier than usual, which was a good thing. It was fun to see the kids who normally didn't consider themselves difference makers making a difference and feeling good about it. We high-fived every kid when we got back in the dugout after an at bat, or after scoring. It's funny – they were telling me and Ricky things like "Watch that second baseman's glove when you're on two, he taps his thigh when there's a pickoff throw," or "I think the ump is giving the pitcher that outside corner, gotta protect a bit more than normal." It was great. Like they had figured out there were other ways to contribute just by being involved, encouraging each other and being a good teammate. Johnny Bench, man. Johnny Bench.

Aside from that, the rest of the game was unremarkable. Ironically, we ended up losing once everyone dropped the antics and just played ball. I didn't like losing, but it was still a fun game, and it didn't bother me as much. Matty though, he was *pissed*, and he wasn't going to be quiet about it.

"This sucks. After all that and those dipsticks are still standing out there like they're the best or something? *Jaysus*," Matty started in as we were grouping up waiting to get in the handshake line. "Man, screw them and their families, I can't believe it……" and he continued with an eloquent yet thoroughly profane rail on the injustice of the whole situation, at least the way he saw it.

When he finished there was a long pause, and one of the grommets said, "Damn dude," which is what we were all thinking. Coach had heard the whole thing - everyone on our side of the diamond had heard it - and he quietly said, "Matty. See that big tree way over there by the other diamond? Go run to it and back. You know why."

We were all standing there in a group watching Matty trot off towards the tree when someone did the unthinkable. A snort. It wasn't like clearing your nose, it was like a stifled snicker. And that's a problem in a group because it's contagious, like a yawn. Especially in this situation because a lot of the team agreed with how Matty felt, and the way he said it was pretty funny. And so the snorts and snickers and throat clearing started to spread around all of us still huddled up there waiting for him to get back.

Coach gave it maybe twelve seconds to see if it would get back under control on its own, but when it did not he finally said," All right you know what? The rest of you go after him. And then form up that handshake line when you all get back, let's go. Let's GO!" So we all started running. As we passed Matty, who was on his way back, he just shook his head at us, but he was grinning.

Afterwards in the handshake line:

"Good game."

"Good game."

"Good game."

"You suck" to my friend Gerry from t-ball on the other team, who said it back to me. We all did this to former teammates and thought it was hilarious. Ricky knew him too and I could hear them exchanging "You suck's" behind me in the line.

"Good game."

"Good game."

The pitcher who got tossed was next, and he pulled his hand when I got there and didn't say anything to me.

I didn't know what to do. This kid was hurt, and apparently it was all my fault. I thought of like five different things I could say but ended up saying nothing. What was the point now? Besides, we lost, and I didn't think you should be running your mouth too much if you didn't win.

"Good game," was all I said to him.

Last guy in line was always the coach. Coach Wilson was a few guys behind me, with Ricky right in front of him, probably on purpose to make sure Ricky didn't start running his mouth too much when he got to the other coach, but he did a bit:

"Good game."

"Ain't no easy outs coach."

"Yeah. Good game."

"Good game."

I think this was a reasonable exception to the "don't talk if you don't win" guideline, and the reaction from their coach was about the only admission or apology he was going to get, but it was good enough.

Ricky and I got on our bikes and headed for home, tossing a red and white plastic mini-football back and forth with Matty and a couple grommets who lived along our route. They usually left on their own and kept quiet around us older guys, but something had changed today, and they were laughing and trying to keep up and play catch with us without crashing and just generally behaving like puppies who finally were allowed to go run with their older siblings. It's not that we didn't want them with us, they just didn't. Usually it was me Ricky and Matty, never really thought about it much but today they rode with us, and every time after that too.

The group thinned out as people went in various

different directions, and we didn't have much time to contemplate or discuss what just happened. Ricky and I had a larger problem we had to solve and a short amount of time we had to do it in.

7

IT SEEMED LIKE A GOOD IDEA AT THE TIME

I suppose if it was simply a matter of matching shattered glass with more shattered glass we could have strategically chucked a rock and been done with it, but that wasn't the point and not really our style anyway. Besides, with the way those big windows ran across the back of the Barlows' kitchen there was no good way to throw anything without a high likelihood of being seen. We had no choice but to get creative. Why do something the simple way if there was a more complicated, dangerous and over-engineered way to do it? That *was* our style, and we were running with it.

We were sitting in Ricky's garage, in the Mustang again. The issue at hand was trying to figure out how to get the stink bomb through the glass and then ignite inside the garage, without either falling off or being incinerated by the rocket before it even got in there.

"A Black Cat maybe? They have extra powder."

"Nah, we've hit windows plenty of times with those accidentally, they're loud but not that much more powerful than Red Rockets or those other ones, the red and blue striped ones."

"Ok ok, so then bigger, the ones with the little red plastic nose cones on them."

"Maybe? Do those blow up though? It's just more flash and sparks, so they leave a trail, I don't think they are that much more powerful. We don't have any of those anyway so can't try it out."

At some point we had decided that we wanted to not only stink bomb the garage, but also blow the whole window out because it would give the stink bomb a better chance of getting through. Plus, he had smashed our window, so we felt like it was the right thing to do. If you're going to do it, might as well go all the way.

Like every other stupid idea we had, this was tricky, and we realized it was going to take some testing to try and work through some kinks and get a better understating of how glass reacted with bottle rockets. Also like every other idea we had, there was a far simpler solution that we were not interested in and were probably going to spend countless hours creating overly complicated and potentially dangerous contraptions and mock-ups.

One of the first hurdles we had to clear was where were we going to try this out, away from the prying eyes of James, parents, and the police, who were already not too keen on us having fireworks in the first place, much less using them to try to blow up windows. We couldn't start blasting rockets at windows around the neighborhood, obviously.

An underground range of some kind would have

been cool as hell, but there aren't a lot of those laying around unused. The alley behind our houses was the best option, but there were a lot of drawbacks. Primarily was the lack of privacy, but we started to realize that maybe it wasn't as bad as we thought.

For one thing, it wasn't your standard "through" alley. There was a big apartment building that ran along most of the street at the far end of the block, and the alley dead-ended there. You could cut through a back yard if you were on foot or bike, but cars couldn't get through. This significantly reduced the amount of traffic in the alley to primarily residents going in and out of their garages, and the garbage men, who were cool with us because we thought they were rad and didn't mess with them.

Another advantage of the alley was that no one would notice what we were up to if we kept the alley looking like … well, an alley. A busted up old window would not attract attention at all. In fact several probably wouldn't. People would assume someone had replaced their old windows or cleaned out the garage or something. There was a spot along the Pavliks' three-flat closer to the apartment building end of the alley that would be good enough. It was sheltered by the side of the building with the least amount of windows, and then there was a big bush and a three car garage on the other side to provide cover, and it was away from our end of the block.

Now we had the "where," but we needed to find targets: windows. No one would notice some broken old wooden sash windows in the garbage in the alley, but they definitely would notice if their garage or house was suddenly missing a window. Ideally, we could find some laying around. People used their garages as places to keep things that they probably didn't need but were also afraid to throw away because "you never know" (my parents and Ricky's dad were of this category). After James Barlow put that brick through the garage window my dad had it fixed in like an hour because he had a spare in the garage. It had been there for seven years waiting for just that moment.

We figured we could liberate a few other old windows from the dusty depths under workbenches or long forgotten in the eaves and rafters. We checked our own garages first, then spread it out. No one would even notice. No more than one window from any location was the original thought, but it turned out we had all the windows we would need from a place no one would ever notice or care.

"What about in here?" Ricky and I were in the alley, and he had stopped behind Mrs. Wild's garage.

Mrs. Wild had a big barn-style garage, right down to the big barn style doors with a board latch across them. It's funny, in all our neighborhood explorations and games of ditch and capture the flag we had been in her garage the least, which make it an outlier because we had been in and out of just about every other garage on the block plenty.

We didn't go in there much because getting in wasn't easy, and when we were doing something that resulted in us needing to go into someone else's garage there usually wasn't a lot of time to mess around. Like the rest of her yard, all around the garage was overgrown with weeds and grass and bushes and whatever. No one had driven a car in or out in years, possibly maybe decades, so it was a little unclear what our best point of entry was.

"It's worth a look I guess. How do you think we should get in?"

There was no way to get in through the big doors without being obvious, and the smaller side door was pretty well jammed shut, as well as being somewhat inaccessible because of all the weeds that had grown up around the garage. There was a window, but it was on the Barlows' side. Somehow it was still intact. I guess James hadn't noticed it yet or just didn't want to put in the effort to smash it out if he knew no one else would notice. Trying to get in through it was not an option.

What we found was that it was quite a lot like an old barn, right down to construction methods, pine boards nailed over stick and post construction, just nails and wood. And over the years, some had started to rot and get loose, and we found a spot that had a bit of both in the alley corner on Ricky's yard side. You had to get under a big lilac bush, and then move one loose board over, and we managed to pry another off but not break it so there was a gap. It wasn't a big gap, but it was big enough for us to crawl through.

The only light came from the Barlow side window and a few open spots in the roof. The floor was dirt, or covered with so much dirt we couldn't tell what was under it. From the looks of things we were the first people who had been in there in a while. It was mostly old gardening tools leaning against one wall, and a long worktable with dust covered cardboard boxes underneath on the other. But leaning against the rear wall we found the motherload.

Stacked on top of each other leaning against the wall were old wood frame plate glass windows. There were large ones at the back, big parlor sized windows, and then decreasing in size all they down to garage window sized in the front, maybe two feet wide by one foot high. Perfect. The nice thing was that these must have been left here after the old double hung windows had been replaced with aluminum storm windows that Mrs. Wild's house had now, so there was no purpose. No one needed them or would miss them. They probably didn't even know they were here anymore.

We briefly considered using her garage for our testing but decided it was too risky, way too close to our target. Plus, there was a lot of old, presumably very dry lumber that the garage was built from and stored in the rafters. One spark or mis-aimed bottle rocket and this whole thing would be up in flames, and people for sure would notice that. But we had our source for test windows, that was the important thing. We also made sure to clear out and try the door from the inside now that we were in here. It was a good spot that not a lot of people knew about, you never knew when it might come in handy.

It didn't take long to learn that glass was a lot harder than we thought. It could survive a direct hit by a standard bottle rocket no problem, they just bounced off, but we knew that already. Then we tried to time the explosion so it would blow just as it approached the window, hoping to maximize the blast radius, but that didn't work the few times we did manage to get it just right. The obvious solution was to move up to a bigger rocket, but that didn't make much of a difference, either. Maybe one of the big boys would have done it, but we didn't have any and those things exploded with a burst which would be counterproductive. This wasn't going to work. By the time we got to something big enough to blow out the window we would practically be shooting a mortar into the garage, and there would be no way to get the stink bomb in if we did that. Plus, shooting something that big into a garage intentionally was on the other side of a line we weren't prepared to cross yet.

I was thinking about all the different ways to launch something – sling shot, throw, compressed air – and it was compressed air that reminded me of Rob Kelton and his piano wire/bb gun/firecracker innovations. It wasn't so much that the rocket wouldn't work, it just needed something to get it through the window, like how the tip on the piano wire stuck in the tree, and then the firecracker blew.

That's how we ended up with one Black Cat "plus powder" bottle rocket taped to a ¼ oz. rocket, with a 1/16 oz. cone-shaped fishing weight (we used them with plastic worms for fishing in the weeds) superglued on the nose and tube smoke bomb underneath. The smoke bomb was our stand-in for the stink bomb. It took numerous attempts and several catastrophic failures on the launchpad to finally start making progress, but we were doing it. The trickiest part was to keep the smoke bomb away from the sparking bottle rocket, so it didn't ignite too early, and the whole thing was severely front heavy, so it had to be fired with a fairly steep launch angle. Also, timing the fuses was difficult. All three had to be lit at the same time, but the rockets had to go first, then a delay, then the smoke bomb. Total time from ignition to explosion, including flight trajectory, had to be around three seconds. We were starting to sound like Hansen with all of this.

Finally, after a couple days of intense trial and error,

arguments, and crude attempts at physics, we blasted a window out, then there was a brief pause, then we saw orange smoke from behind. It was everything we hoped for, except for a cinematic fireball, but we had crossed off all the technical requirements and that was more aesthetic, so we let it go and took the win.

There were a couple of final issues to solve. Because of the combined rocket size, we needed to be a little farther away from the target garage than we had previously thought would be necessary, so we couldn't launch it from Mrs. Wild's back yard using the birthday candle method again. We needed at least another twenty feet (straight line) and then we had to get clear airspace, and that was going to be trouble too because there was that row of pine trees along the property line between Ricky's house and Mrs. Wild's, so if we were going to launch from Ricky's yard somewhere we were going to have to somehow go over or through those. We had one chance to get this lined up just right and no real way to dial it in because we couldn't take any test shots at the Barlows' garage without tipping our hand. We were going to be relying on a lot of things going right in a very specific way at a very specific time. As usual.

The specific time was going to be the Fourth of July. Really there's no better day to launch a fireworks attack. Way too much other stuff being shot off, so it would make it very difficult to pinpoint the origins of any one particular shot that could be traced back to us. James might be able to sniff it out but unless we were careless or got spotted setting things up it was the perfect cover.

Setting up the launch pad wasn't too bad because we had gained some experience with this set up and were starting to get the hang of it. We had to keep the rocket area concealed, and since we were using the candle method, shielded from the wind. We ended up under Ricky's deck. There was just enough space to get the angle of elevation we needed at launch, and we thought there was a decent enough gap in the line of pine trees that we could thread the needle and get the rocket through.

Even though it was under a deck, it still needed camouflage or else anyone looking under would be able to see. Fortunately, there was enough yard-and-garden type stuff Ricky's stepmom had around that we could use. A couple over-sized ceramic pots, some pavers stacked up just right and we were good. All we had to do now was wait until it got dark on the Fourth.

8

FOURTH OF JULY: THE BEGINNING

It was overcast when I woke up, but according to the radio it was going to clear, and if there was any rain it would be out of the area well before lunchtime. That was fine then, the cookouts and picnics were still going to happen. The parade would still happen. The All-Star game would still happen. Fireworks would still happen.

The Fourth of July was different than the other holidays. If you looked past the ridiculous amounts of illegal fireworks, it was kind of sweet and wholesome, if short-lived. For one day it really was hot dogs, apple pies and baseball, which was a strange and rare thing to experience although I didn't know it at the time. Here we were in a large urban suburb of a major US city, and yet it transformed into a Norman Rockwell painting that came out for this one holiday, and then once the fireworks had all blown off everyone just packed it all up and put it away until next year.

Almost every house had an American flag hanging,

including ours. Lots of the big old Victorians on the north side of town put up red, white, and blue bunting or streamers. There was a parade in the morning with fire trucks and floats that people would throw candy off to the crowd, who were all lined up waving little American flags.

Every year my mom made chocolate cupcakes with white frosting, and then she gave me and my brother red and blue frosting we would help decorate them with. The neighbors looked forward to them every year, so she made a lot. Everyone was going to be in their back yards grilling and sharing stuff over the fence. Sometimes it would spill out the front yards depending on how your neighborhood was.

It was the biggest day for block parties. It was easy to get a permit and then they would let you block off the street with barricades and the whole block would be out there. Volleyball nets stretched across the street, kids riding bikes and setting up ramps, squirt guns, water balloons. All the guys would bring their grills out to the front yards, and coolers full of beers. I think it ended up causing a lot of traffic problems because there were so many streets closed off, so they ended up limiting the amount of permits available because there definitely were less in later years, but this year it was in full effect.

Our block had a block party, and it was fantastic, but not on the Fourth of July. We still all got out there, just not "officially" and it was pretty fun, although for the most part daytime on the Fourth was mostly about killing time until it got dark.

This year was different because I was going to be playing in the All-Star game for the first time. A lot of my extended family was going to be there, so we were going to be having a gathering at our house. My aunts and uncles were all older than me, but not so much older that they still didn't have their trophies in their rooms displayed. They understood this was a big deal and they wanted to be there at the game for me. I don't even think my parents came to regular games. Maybe once in a while, but not often. My mom was there when we were younger, but part of that was because someone had to get us to and from practice, and another part was she was friends with a lot of the other moms anyway, so it was kind of a socializing opportunity for them.

It was my first All-Star game and my last year playing league ball. If I wanted to continue with organized baseball, I would have had to try out for Pony league which was like a travelling thing, and basically like minor league for high school ball if that makes sense, and I wasn't sure about playing in high school anyway. Ricky said the coach had already reached out to him, asking if he would try out but even Ricky didn't want to make that kind of commitment, and he was more interested in wrestling anyway. We were both fine with it, now seemed like a good time to make an exit.

I finished my cereal and left to go check out the parade. It went down Washington Boulevard, which was two blocks south, the far end of the lot that Emerson school was on. As I headed out the front door I heard "Hey Peaches, happy Fourth of July!" from somewhere over my head. It was the neighbors, the Smedleys. They lived next door to us in a brick two flat just like ours that had a nice flat roof. I had been up on ours with my dad a couple times and had contemplated if it would be possible to jump from roof to roof. All three brick two-flats were carbon copies of each other, so all had flat roofs, but they also had concrete driveways in between and it looked like a long way down from up there, so I never tested the idea.

I squinted up from the porch and I could see Billy and Charlie up above me on their roof. "Hey guys happy Fourth! Going to the parade?" I called up to them.

"Nah think we're going to watch from up here. See you later, have fun!"

They waved their beers at me (it was just after 8am) and I headed out. As I got to the corner I heard the unmistakable whizz BANG of a bottle rocket behind me. I looked back and those two knuckleheads were laughing and waving and holding a piece of conduit. I smiled and waved. I didn't think much of the fact that my next-door neighbors were on the roof with unknown amounts of alcohol and fireworks and shot a bottle rocket at me. They were younger guys, they had big parties sometimes, they had a hot tub, it was not out of character for them. It was a nice day to be on the roof – overcast, not too hot yet, probably a nice breeze up there.

"Peaches! Wait up!" Ricky came trotting up "I heard the State Farm float is going to be throwing those little footballs."

"You don't have enough already?"

"No. I roofed two, and the dog ate one so I'm down to one and I don't feel like going over to the office and getting more."

"You could just go for a ride by Matty's house."

"What? Why?"

"Nothing, never mind. Let's go"

Ricky was also going to be playing in the All-Star game, but it was not his first. I'm pretty sure he made it every year. I didn't know if I was going to be starting, but I knew he was. It occurred to me that all the times we had played together whether it was in the neighborhood, or at Emerson, or even in leagues I had never really felt like I was part of that group of "good" that he was in. Now we were both All-Stars. Best kids on all the teams were playing today and I was going.

Ricky must have known what I was thinking. "Ready for the game today? This is going to be a good one. There's a pitcher for American Foods, that big dude, that I heard is getting scouted." I knew who he was talking about, and his name was Mike Dobbs. We were friends, in the same class at school and had been for years. He came from a big family, and he was on the tail end of it so it was all older brothers and sisters for him.

Mike was a big guy, at least for our age group. He was a full foot taller than me and was solid. He didn't play any sports besides baseball and football, and he had kinda the same approach to both, overwhelm opponents with size and power. I never played football, but I heard stories about him steamrolling dudes frequently.

We were never on the same team, he was in the Southside league, but I had seen him play back in our younger days. He had that "big league" swing even then, a big upward arching full body committed power blast. He wasn't pitching that game, but I knew what he could do back then I imagined it had only improved. I'm glad Ricky was confident because it made me a little less intimidated.

"Who else you think got in for Southside? You know

Nubby and Mark B. from Citizens Bank are going. Oh, and that catcher from Polly Dry Cleaners, that kid who threw out Tricky Nick that one time."

Tricky Nick was on our team, utility guy who could serviceably play several positions, and he was the shiftiest baserunner in the league. He was fast, sure, but he also had a quality that could not be replicated. He was completely unpredictable. It was barely controlled chaos when he was on the bases. He would be standing on the bag at first chatting with the first baseman who was holding him there. The pitcher would get set, first baseman would get off the bag to play defense and Tricky Nick would just walk out there with him, still chatting. And then just keep going, like a casual stroll over to second base. He didn't walk the whole way, but he was just so relaxed and natural about it that it took the other team a minute to react to him casually stealing and then he would take off, going from easy paced walk to full sprint to headfirst slide in what seemed like all one motion. Nick didn't do it all the time, but he had plenty of other moves, too. He really could not be held to a base if he decided he was stealing.

Everyone in the league knew Tricky Nick, or at least knew what he was capable of, especially the pitchers. We were really happy to have him on our team, but it was pure coincidence because he lived on the other side of town. If it weren't for how they divided up the borders, we would have had to play against him. It was strange, but because of the way the boundaries were drawn, even though Ricky and I were Southside kids, we played for the Northside.

The Northside of town was the side with the big old houses, big lawns. Some famous writers and architects and businessmen grew up there. Plenty of CEOs and Notre Dame grads, it had an old money feel. Later in high school these were the kids who got new Mercedes for their 16th birthday. They were the rich kids with the best stuff; the latest clothes we couldn't afford, summer trips to lake houses, going to colleges we couldn't get into.

I'm not saying it was substandard living conditions where we lived on the Southside at all. It was still nice, but you could see the difference. We had smaller houses, and they were closer together. There were apartment buildings running east down Washington all the way to Austin Boulevard. I think "working class" would be a fair description. People hung their laundry outside to dry, dads were working on cars over beers in the garage on Saturday after cutting the grass. Most of our friends and the kids we went to school with all played on Southside teams, except Matty who got caught up in the same boundary line issue we did.

So, it was a little conflicting for us. We played for the Northside, but we were rooting for the Southside. Kinda. We wanted to win whenever we played so we weren't about to do anything to sabotage the game, but there was a bit of a Civil War/brother vs brother action we could feel for sure. I suppose it was very much like being in the pros and playing for wherever you got drafted or traded to or signed, at least that's how we rationalized it. The businesses that sponsored the teams were almost all on the north side, so we didn't shop there very often and neither did our parents. Our teammates were cool though. I don't think I ever had any issue with anyone talking down or pulling rank or anything like that. We were all there to play baseball, and the diamond is a great equalizer.

"That first baseman from Cunningham-Reiley probably. Name's 'Gino' I think?"

"Oh yeah! Remember when he almost did the splits and got me? He's good."

"For sure. I hope Diego and Kelly are playing. They're on Citizen's this year right? They live over by Paulie only further north, cool guys."

We had made it to our spot and joined the other folks lining the street waiting for the parade. Little kids with sparklers and flags sitting on the curb, some kids with legal fireworks (snap-n-pops and snakes mostly, not a good environment for smoke bombs) on the sidewalks behind them. We hung back with the parents and other bigger kids in the grass and watched the fire engines roll by lights on and sirens going. The bank float with the person dressed in a lion suit went by. Ricky got his footballs from the insurance agency float. High school marching bands with mascots and cheerleaders. The police on horses, and then a couple guys with shovels to clean up anything the horses might have left brought up the rear.

The parade was over, and we were walking back home, tossing a red and white mini-football back and forth. There were still a few hours until gametime, so we were planning on hanging in the neighborhood for a bit, having something to eat and then riding our bikes over to Hillgrove Commons together. We crossed the street at the end of our block and heard the distinct hiss of a bottle rocket and then BANG over our heads.

"Happy Fourth guys ahahahahaha" from up on the roof. The Smedley brothers, still at it.

"Those guys are going to be a lot of fun by tonight,"

Ricky said smiling and waving up at them.

"They've lived there for what 6 years now and never gone on the roof before? I wonder what made them think of it this year."

"I think the beer played a large part in that decision."

Hiss BANG - another bottle rocket.

"Hey, hey guys, my girlfriend got the grill going out back, you guys stop by and grab a hot dog, ok? Did your mom make cupcakes again this year?" Charlie was waving at us while the other one was readying another rocket. We didn't really care that they were nonchalantly shooting at us while having a conversation. It wasn't the first time we had been shot at. Me and Ricky shot bottle rockets at each other every now and then so no harm no foul. These were just the little guys anyway, more noise than anything else. What we didn't know was that the Smedleys had gone to Indiana and absolutely loaded up with whatever rockets they could get their hands on, and it was all up there on the roof with them. They were just warming up right now.

"She did. I'll bring over a plate and grab a dog, thanks guys! Happy Fourth!" I yelled up.

Hiss BANG!

"Thank you! Hahahahaha."

Ricky was right, they were having a good time already but give those guys a few more hours up there and it was going to get really good.

9

ALL-STAR GAME

Baseball is notoriously superstitious. Any positive or negative outcome that can somehow be linked to what seems like an unrelated action or object is taken seriously at every level, all the way up to the big leagues. No stepping on foul lines when going out to or coming in from the field. Do not talk to the starting pitcher before his start. If a pitcher has a no hitter going, do not acknowledge it in any way to anyone, and do not acknowledge the pitcher's existence. I have seen guys who were in the middle of a no-hitter sitting by themselves at the end of the bench completely alone, the rest of the team huddled at the other end of the dugout.

Batters had their own set of rituals based on superstition. Adjust your gloves an exact number of times, touch your belt, heart and head in a particular order. Tap the corners of the plate in a particular order or certain number of times. The bat itself was sometimes treated like a sacred object, protected in a special place, only to be used by one person. Or the opposite would happen and everyone had to use "the Bat" so it would continue to fuse the team's power and get hits.

If you had a good game, you would eat the same pre-game meal before the next game. Some guys believe in the power of apparel and don't wash uniforms or socks if they were on a hot streak. Getting a new glove could be a dangerous proposition – if it wasn't broken in just right, not only physically but spiritually, you could be dealing with grounders through the legs, dropped pop-ups or who knows what. That glove needed to be oiled, have a hard ball put in the web and wrapped with rubber bands, then put under your mattress for a week before it ever saw any use.

Some of these, like the no stepping on the chalk lines and no talking to a pitcher during a no-hitter, were generally accepted as part of baseball's unwritten rules, of which there are many. Some of the other stuff, while I didn't discourage it or speak against it, I can't say that I believed wearing a certain hat or tapping the plate a number of times would make a difference in how I played.

Pregame meal though, that was serious. Campbell's Chunky Soup. When I first started playing fast pitch, my practices were all the way on the north side of town, about as far north as you could go, which was roughly 4 miles from my house. I had to leave pretty early to get there on time since I was riding my bike, so my mom wanted to get something easy that I could handle making for myself. Campbell's Chunky Soup it was, and for whatever reason it stuck. I would not play a game without getting my soup. Didn't matter if the game was at 9 am, I was having a hot bowl of soup.

So that's what I was doing at 10:40 in the morning on the Fourth of July, wearing my uniform eating soup at the kitchen table, carefully. Because we were going to be the home team, our All-Star jerseys were white. I didn't mind getting dirty during the game but I'm not showing up pre-stained. My dad might have said something to my mom and my brother because no one was talking around me. On some level I now understood what it was like to be the pitcher during a no-hitter. It was all business. I was focused on…well nothing actually. A strange feeling of being disconnected had come over me while I was putting on that All-Star uniform. I almost felt like I was watching me do things, like I was a passenger in my head just along for the ride. I was a little nervous too.

It turned out Ricky had to go do some family stuff, so I was going to catch up with him at the field, which left me to further explore my own head on the ride over to Hillgrove Commons. It was quiet in there today. I suppose my thoughts were more focused on fireworks and other nighttime activities or maybe I was just enjoying the day too much to get super nervous yet. Mostly I was concerned about messing up in front of all the other guys. Also, this was part of the end of line for me with organized baseball and I was just enjoying things that maybe I had been too focused on other aspects of the game to notice. It felt different now that I was one of the "older guys" passing on what I could to the next crop of grommets. I couldn't remember if we were that small when we started in the league? I think kids were shrinking or something.

This calm thoughtfulness ended when I went under the viaduct on East Avenue and turned to look at the field. It was incredible. The park district had set up extra rows of bleachers, so now there was like three times as much seating. Sponsor's banners and flags and bunting hung along the dugouts. They had music playing from speakers, and an actual announcer's booth! Some of the costumed mascots from the parade where there working the crowd, running around on the diamond and entertaining the little kids. I had only been to a couple minor league games, but it very much felt like those minor league ball parks. They even had a vendor walking through the bleachers selling hot dogs out of one of those metal boxes.

Now I got a little more nervous. I had never played in front of this many people, and in this kind of atmosphere. It was like "real" baseball, more real than I had ever experienced as a player anyway. My stomach did some flip flops, and I was grateful there was nothing more than soup down there.

I locked my bike at the end of the rack. This was another superstition, only this one was also based on the fact that James Barlow had stolen the original wheels off my bike and if I used the end of the rack I could get the chain through both of the tires. Bike secured, I took my glove off the handlebars and headed over to our side of the field. I recognized the head coach for our team. It was the first coach I had on the first team I played for in fastpitch, Pete "Smell It" Helman. I didn't know he was going to be coaching today, and I was glad to see him.

Pete was a character. He and his two friends – Captain Rick who always wore aviator sunglasses and

Jim the Jimbo - were great guys who I had learned quite a lot from. I never knew what they did outside of practice and games or where they lived, where they worked, even if they were married or not. They were clearly good friends and they loved baseball and it occurred to me later in life that there was also a gambling aspect to baseball that perhaps was in play here as well, but not in an ominous way, just making it a little more interesting for each other. I think all the coaches were friends or at least friendly acquaintances, played league softball sponsored by the sports bars they hung out in and just liked sports in general. They reminded me a lot of my next-door neighbors the Smedleys.

Pete was big on fundamentals and doing things the right way, which we responded to because we loved Johnny Bench and Pete Rose, and they loved fundamentals and doing things the right way too. We broke down everything in infield and outfield drills. Catch with two hands, no hot dogging, don't care what you see the pros do. If you fielded a grounder with one hand when you could have used two you were running laps, and if you did it in a game you were warned and then benched if it happened again. Always run it out to first base, even if it's an easy infield grounder. Defensive batting, working a count, when to bunt were among the many things we learned from Pete and the other two coaches.

It seemed kinda nitpicky sometimes I guess, but it definitely won us some games. There were a lot of kids who came from t-ball that just didn't have all the tools yet and his methods, and focus on fundamentals like solid fielding, smart batting, and teamwork gave a lot of them a better foundation and some confidence. Plus, he was right, if you work hard at the basics, master them, statistically you will be better.

His nickname, "Smell It," came from his affection for the hit-and-run, and his unique way of calling it out. The hit-and-run play usually goes like this: When there is a runner on first, the first baseman is forced closer to the bag to hold the runner, leaving a larger gap on that side of the infield. This also means the shortstop and the second baseman are going to have to cover second base if there's a steal attempt. So, you have the runner take off like he's going to steal, but the hitter makes contact, essentially giving the runner a massive jump, as well as taking advantage of the big gaps in the infield.

This is a high risk, high reward play, and the risk part is all on the batter. He *must* make contact. Ideally the batter gets the ball through one of the gaps in the infield, which would score the runner. Less ideal but still effective, a grounder that is fielded forces an infielder to make the throw to first and eliminates a double play opportunity, leaving the lead runner on second with no force out at third. It was a crazy, risky play that really required you to focus on your job and trust your teammates and we loved it just as much as Pete did.

In theory, it was a great play and smart, situational baseball strategy. In reality, it hardly ever worked, but Pete loved hit-and-runs, and you could count on him trying it at least once per game. He was also a master of determining when the other team was going to try one. This is where his nickname came from. If we were in the field and he thought the opposing team was going to try a hit-and-run he would yell out *"I smell it!"* and we knew to get ready. We actually picked off quite a few runners that way. Pete was a good coach, and I was glad he was here.

"Peaches! You ready to have some fun today?" This is what Pete said to every one of his players before every game. He was grinning at me.

He wasn't quite as tall as I remembered, but it was still my guy Pete. Handshake and back tap one arm hug, "Hey coach! How have you been?"

"Great! Congrats on being here bud, took you long enough," he teased but I could see he was proud.

"Yeah it did. Thanks" We both stood looking at each other for a second, and then we both felt dumb, and I smirked. Pete rolled his eyes.

"You know what, get out there and get loose with everyone else before we start getting all emotional."

"Yes *sir!*" We were both laughing now.

I knew, or at least knew of, most of the kids in the outfield. They were the best on their teams, we always talked pregame about how to work around them or what to watch out for. It was cool we were all on the same side today. John McNamara, my old t-ball teammate and current teammate, a solid third baseman and excellent hitter. Eddie White and Chris DeSault who played first and second base for Rand Insurance were there, double play specialists. A couple of other kids said "hey" and we were all just tossing around baseballs and goofing. Now it felt like I had made it. I can't truthfully say that I never cared about making the All-Star team or winning trophies or games. I did care.

Coach Pete whistled and waved us in. "Everybody huddle up, huddle up." We bunched up along the third base line on the foul side of the bag past the dugout. "Ok guys welcome to the All-Star Game.

Congratulations to each one of you on being here, it is a great honor, and it is my honor to be your coach for this game. Assisting me today are Coach Wilson and Coach Armstrong. I'm not going to take a lot of time making a speech here, so let's get a few things out of the way; first, everyone is going to get a chance to play. If you do not start you will be in probably around the third or fourth inning. Pitchers get one inning each maximum otherwise your coaches will accuse me of trying to wear you out (laughter). Nah I'm kidding, I got seven pitchers here I need to work in so let's cooperate, please throw strikes (more laughter). We'll keep the signs simple," and he looked over at the other dugout real quick and then motioned Coach Wilson to stand behind him, blocking their view.

"Ok, here we go," and he both told and made the signs for us:

"Hand across my chest left to right is the indicator, anything before that is acting.

Left ear and right ear tug – take.

Pat the top of the hat and wipe the brim – swing away.

Tap right bicep twice – bunt.

Touch the nose – hit and run.

Wipe down both forearms and swing – steal."

Pete went through all of them again and then aggressively wiggled his belt buckle.

"Coach what was that one? What does that mean again?"

"It means my nuts itch." This busted everyone out. If he had planned it as an icebreaker, it worked. You could feel the tension ease.

"One more thing and then we'll get lineups and

batting order. A lot of people say the All-Star game is an exhibition, a showcase, something for the fans and parents and the league sponsors. And they are right. It's for fun, but if you aren't aware the Southside has won the last four years, and I think it would be extra fun if we ended that streak here today, and I'll tell ya, with this group, I think we can do it. You guys are the best, let's go show everyone that ok? *Ok? Fun time on 3 one two three…"*

"FUN TIME!" we all yelled.

We all lined up in front of our dugouts and took off out hats for the National Anthem, that was cool, and then Coach Wilson told us the starting lineup (I was not starting) and batting order. Since we were the "home" team for the game we would be taking the field first so the guys ran out to their positions, infielders tossing around a ball, then over to the pitcher who took a few warmup pitches before the catcher yelled out "coming down" to let second base know he was throwing a pickoff.

Coaches shook hands, gave the ump their batting orders, then he *yelled "Play ball!"* and motioned over to the batter in the visitors on-deck circle. Game time.

Our starting pitcher was Carlos from Rand Insurance. Not the nastiest but he was consistent and accurate, could throw hard and most importantly could get away with a sneaky breaking ball once in a while. In the big leagues, usually the pitchers have the advantage. Down here at our level, not so much. It was against the rules to throw curves or anything breaking. Allegedly if the ump or opposing coach caught you throwing one you could be kicked out of the game, although none of us had ever seen that happen. However, this did limit pitchers to only throwing fastballs and changeups and maybe sneak a breaking ball in if they could disguise the spin and keep their delivery the same. For the most part though the batter had a slight edge. I say slight, but it was very dependent upon the pitcher and the situation.

I'm not sure if the coaches talked or if it was an All-Star game thing or what (this was an exhibition game after all) because the second pitch Carlos threw was a beauty of a breaking ball that confused the batter so bad it seemed like he had time to take another swing before the ball actually got to the catcher, he swung that early. All the ump said was "steeeeEEEERIKE ONE," so I guess it was cool for the pitchers to throw whatever junk they could think up, and that was fine with us. More than fine, actually, we *wanted* to see that, we wanted to know what it was like facing it. My coaches would throw me curves in batting practice just for fun, but honestly they weren't as good as some of these pitchers. Besides, we thought that rule was stupid anyway.

Usually when I was on the bench in the dugout I just goofed with my friends while we watched the game and cheered on my teammates. In between the action there was much discussion about equipment: what was the best bat in the bag, which batting helmet smelled the worst, why Joe's new glove sucked. There was not much discussion about that now though. The announcer disrupted the conversation, but it sounded like he was in a different room or something. They had the portable speakers for the PA pointed away from us on the field and towards the crowd so we just heard muffled mush mouth and sometimes we could recognize a name or a position:

"Scrmnaff Humple farff NoooOOOOObalob Jimmeh Reilllleeehhhh famfonom hermanermanon…"

We were having a blast just trying to decipher what this guy was saying, making up our own stuff, not paying too much attention to the game itself from a player's perspective. There was just way too much going on to focus on the game. Those of us who didn't start were kinda spectating and there really wasn't much reason to get strategic anyway, the game was very back-and-forth but the teams seemed pretty evenly matched. It made sense, the All-Star game was the best players, so we were seeing the absolute best pitchers, and they knew they were only going to have to throw for an inning, so they were just letting it rip. More than one kid came back to the dugout shaking his head. It was fun to watch though, and there was still some breakthrough offense that kept things interesting.

TOP OF THE FOURTH

By now the score was tied up at 2-2. Coach Wilson said it was time for some of the starters to come out.

"Peaches, center field, batting in the three spot, after Nick."

The tightness in my chest and rumbling in my stomach, which had subsided since the start of the game, returned with renewed intensity. This is it, actually playing in the All-Star game. In front of all these people. Please don't let me mess up here.

I grabbed my glove off the bench and trotted out, carefully stepping over the third base foul line, and headed across the infield toward center. My parents claim this was a big moment for them and my aunts and uncles in the stands and they all cheered when they saw me heading out, but I have zero recollection of this.

Everything that was not happening on the field just …faded into the background. I was focused on the game and more importantly not screwing it up, which right now was a bit of a battle I was having with my nerves.

In left was Davey Martinez. I had known Davey off and on over the years, never on the same team but played against each other plenty of times, he was solid and fast as hell. He had the ball and tossed it to me, and I turned and tossed it over to Big Roy in right field. Also a good dude, played for Star Dry Cleaners. Roy was not fast as hell, but he was big as hell. He was really strong and could make the throw from the outfield to the plate without one hopping it no problem. His problem was mobility. Once he got going he was a mover, but it just took all that mass an extra second to get in gear.

We had a minute or two more than usual to toss the ball because the ump was giving pitchers a few extra warm up throws since they were rotating in and out so often, but then I heard Matty yell from behind the plate "Coming down!" He was taking a practice pickoff throw to second and then it would get tossed around the infield, ending at the shortstop who would walk it in and hand it to the pitcher. Another baseball tradition.

Second base was responsible for covering the bag, and center field was responsible for backing him up, but I wasn't too worried about it. I knew Matty could make that throw because I had seen him make it plenty of times, so I jogged in a bit and stood behind the base while the throw came in perfectly and then jogged back out to my position.

Center field is like the captain of the outfield. Left is where all the action is and right is usually where you put the space cases. It was my job to back up all plays, fill in gaps, tell those guys to back up or move in or shift left or right. I could call anyone off a fly ball, even infielders. I didn't really expect to have to do much though. This was the All-Star game, and while I hadn't played with the two guys out there with me before, I wasn't worried. There hadn't been a whole lot of deep hits so far, and these two were pretty decent so I felt like we had it covered.

I was right about part of it anyway, but very wrong about the number of hits. Batters were getting warmed up, as well as getting used to the speed and movement of the pitches and just the atmosphere in general. Guys started to dial it in and we were busy in the outfield. It's not that the pitchers were doing worse or going through the order so hitters were seeing them 2 or 3 times, they were bringing in a fresh pitcher every inning. I guess all that potential for offense finally broke through because we were running our asses off out there. It was great. This was turning into a real game, and Pete was right, we were having fun.

BOTTOM OF THE FIFTH

Bottom of the fifth inning, the score was now 5-4 with Southside up. I was in the on-deck circle getting loose. Some guys like to use two bats for warm up swings, some guys like to use the doughnut weight that goes down on to the barrel of the bat. I didn't really like either one, I preferred to just take easy swings, maybe watch the pitcher, and try to get the timing down a bit. It was more of a mental thing for me, trying to focus on seeing the ball, not deviate my swing form, keep it loose, look for good pitches and try to get good read on where the ball was coming out of the pitcher's hand.

The current batter, Tricky Nick, hit a sputtering, spinning grounder that the shortstop managed to knock down but couldn't get the throw over to first before Nick dug it out and got there, safe. Man on first, one out, I'm up.

I heard the announcer say, "Now bobbbbingggg for the Nerfsiiiibe tartars, Peebaaah Jupidahhhh" and there was a muffled cheer but then I was all business. Checked down the line to the third base coach and got the sign. Take.

I stepped in the box and the pitcher went into the stretch. Tricky Nick had a four-step lead off first base and had his hands out on both sides of him like he was balancing there, knees bent, staring at the pitcher. He was daring him.

The pitcher went into his windup and threw. I wasn't swinging, but I could see it was coming in about shoulder high and outside. Out of the corner of my eye I saw movement. Crap, the catcher was getting up! It was a pitchout. They were trying to catch Nick far enough off the bag with a throw down from the catcher. I guess they really wanted him off the bases.

Nick knew I was taking the pitch, and he wasn't planning on going anywhere anyway, so he just dove back to first base when he saw the catcher getting up and beat the throw. He got up, dusting the dirt off his uniform with a grin. Pete said something into Nick's ear. Now Nick was really grinning.

I looked down the third base line for the sign. Take, again. Nothing weird about that, the count was 1-0, might as well see if he can put one over for a strike with Nick being such a distraction out there. This time Nick had a huge lead, maybe five steps off the base. The first baseman wasn't even moving off the bag, he was standing there covering with his glove up.

Pitcher went into the stretch, looking over his left shoulder at first and Nick. He spun and threw over to first. Nick was quick enough to get back under the tag, but it was close. Again, he got up dusting himself off, both him and Pete grinning like they had some kind of inside joke going on over there.

I checked back down to third for the sign before stepping in. Still "take." Pitcher went into the stretch again, and Nick had a good lead. After looking over his shoulder for about six seconds, he wound up and threw. It was a good fastball, but outside. Ball two. Nick just jogged back to first and stood there waiting for the sign. I looked down at Coach Wilson. He gave his left ear and right ear a tug, "take" again. I was getting a little frustrated, but I understood the strategy behind it. I really wanted to swing, but in this situation, you have to let the pitcher throw. If he misses again, the count is 3-0. I wasn't super thrilled about drawing a walk, but on base is on base I guess; however you end up getting there shouldn't matter. I still wanted a hit in the All-Star game though.

The pitcher really stared Nick down this time. Again, Nick walked out to a good-sized lead, and again they had a stare down, but the pitcher wound up and threw a smoking fastball, right down the pipe. Strike one. The count was now 2-1.

Instead of throwing the ball back to the pitcher, the catcher got up and walked it to the mound so he could have a quick chat. I stood off to the third base side of the plate, taking it all in for a minute. I assumed they were discussing the best strategy for them to get out of this spot. They could try to either keep Nick on first and get me out or try to pick him off. Their biggest concern was that if I got a hit there was a good chance Nick could score, he was that fast. For me, there was the risk of hitting into a double play, so if at all possible I was going to try and keep it off the ground, but with this pitcher that was going to be tough.

The catcher jogged back from the mound and got down behind the plate. I checked down to third base for the sign. Coach Wilson tapped the side of his nose.

Hit and run.

Hit and run?

For real, Pete?

C'mon man. I mean, he tried them all the time, so it wasn't out of character, but why now and why me? I just wanted to get a hit, play the game, have some fun…

I glanced over at Pete and Nick at first, ready to glare at them, and they were both just looking at me smirking. Something in my train of thought just flipped over on itself. They weren't making a joke at my expense; they were making me part of it. I stopped thinking about getting my hit and everyone watching and all that and instead thought, "You know what...why not? What the hell, let's give it a shot. Let's have some fun." I mean, why couldn't we? I was becoming more amused than anything else, and suddenly I didn't care so much. I wasn't indifferent about it, I cared, but I didn't at the same time. I wasn't worried about what might happen, I wanted to see what was going to happen, because I was just having fun now. It was like the best game that didn't matter at all. I wasn't even nervous anymore, that all just dissolved away.

This is what Pete and Nick were doing over there,

setting it all up. Pete was looking right at me smiling, Nick was smiling and looking calm, and when I stepped into the box he took about a four-step lead. Again, the first baseman held the bag, second base shifted over more into the gap, there was a huge hole in the right field side of the infield.

Pitcher went into the stretch, again staring Nick down hard over his left shoulder. A quick spin and throw over to first, but Nick was back in time, safe.

The pitcher collected himself and went into the stretch, trying to keep Nick on the bag with his stare, again. I guess he was satisfied because he went into the windup, and Nick took off. We were about to find out if statistics and probability were with us or against us today.

The way a properly executed hit and run plays out is actually the reverse of its name. The first thing that happens is "run" and that's what Nick was doing. Now it was all up to me. If I didn't make contact, he was probably going to be thrown out at second because the second baseman was already moving that way to cover the bag, leaving an even bigger hole in the right side of the infield. *Please don't let me mess this up*, I thought.

Fastball low, possibly a bit outside. If you're going to be late on contact with a fastball, what happens is you pull it, and it goes to the opposite field. I was pretty comfortable hitting in any direction, and I wanted it to go to the opposite field, so all I tried to do was take a nice easy swing, get the bat on the ball and hope it doesn't push too much and go foul.

It did not go foul. I got it to drop in right field, just where the second baseman's head would have been had he not been over the bag waiting for a throw that never came. Right and center fielders were deep to prevent me from getting one past them, so it landed in kind of no-man's land out there. I took off for first. That was all I was focused on now, getting to the base.

I could see the right fielder reach the ball at a dead sprint, pick it up and throw to his cutoff man but I didn't see what happened after that because I was afraid he would got to first and get me. I was still about two steps away from being safe so I put my head down and ran hard, hearing Pete say, "Hold up, hold up here," as I crossed the bag, turning to the right so I was out of the basepath. Safe.

As I jogged back to first, I saw that Nick was on third. I guess that right fielder had a better arm than we all assumed and got the ball back to the infield before Nick could get home. So now it was runners on first and third, one out. The tying run, Tricky Nick, was on third. The go ahead run, me, was on first. But there was still a possible double play with the force out at second now, and I was pretty sure I knew what Pete was going to tell me to do.

The Southsiders had called time and were having a little meeting on the pitcher's mound, giving me and Pete a chance to talk. "Good work, way to make contact, knew you were the right man for the plan. You have to steal second, I want to try to squeeze Nicky home."

Pete had apparently decided to just dump out the whole bag of plays right here, right now. The steal I expected, the squeeze I did not, for good reason. The suicide squeeze is a very specific type of hit-and-run. You have a runner on third, and the batter bunts down the first base line. The runner goes on the pitch, squeezing into home before there's a play. Hopefully. It is incredibly risky, and there's more ways that things can go wrong than ways things that can go right.

If the hitter can't get the bunt down, the runner is almost certainly out. If he does get the bunt down but it dies near the plate, runner is out. If he's not fast enough you can experience the humiliation of a failed squeeze double play, where the runner is tagged out at home and then throw to first beats the runner there, which would make outs number two and three and that would end the inning. There was a lot that needed to happen for this to work.

At the same time, I understood what Pete was doing and why he was doing it now. "Nowwwww rabblih fwahhhhhhmahe Morpsizzzze Allsawssssss, John Magnawawahhhhhh!" Johnny Mac, my buddy from t-ball days and current teammate on Olsen Foods was stepping up to bat. Everyone knew he was a power hitter. I had played with him for years and had never seen him bunt outside of bunting practice. No one would be expecting it, so we had the element of surprise on our side. The drawback was that I didn't know how much of a speed burst John could sustain, so there was a good chance he could be thrown out if this bunt didn't go exactly right.

"You sure? John could probably hit a sacrifice fly and get him in." The meeting on the mound was over and the first baseman was trotting back over towards us.

Pete shrugged. He was still grinning. "Nah, I want to do it this way. Trust me, it'll be fun. Get ready, get your sign."

Take, and no steal.

Nick, on third, trickled out to a lead. Since the

pitcher was a righty, he was looking directly at him through his entire stretch and windup so Nick couldn't get quite as frisky as he was on first, but he still had a good lead. Pitcher stepped off and Nick side shuffled three times back to the bag. He was playing it casual, and for all I knew this kind of situation *was* casual for Nick. He lived for stuff like this and probably wasn't in much of a hurry for things to unfold.

I was just holding the bag, the pitcher turned and looked at me before he turned his back and stepped back on the rubber. John stepped into the box. I took a three-step lead even though I wasn't going anywhere. It's funny; all three of us were acting like something was going to happen when we knew nothing was going to happen, and the other team, especially in the infield, was starting to get a little tense from the slow but deliberate pressure Pete's strategies were applying to them. Very aware of their positions and our positions. No infield chatter.

The pitcher let it rip. John started to pick up his front leg like the start of his swing but held the bat as a fastball just at the knees went by him for strike one. I jogged back to first and touched the base. Nick was standing on third. John looked down for the sign before stepping onto the batter's box. Take, and steal. Showtime.

John stepped in the box and Nick took another good-sized lead down third base line. I shuffled out about two and a half steps. I noticed that second baseman was not moving over towards the bag to cover. Like not at all. He was just sitting out there in between first and second, which was weird because the first baseman was moving off the bag on the pitch so he could cover anything coming down the first base line.

They were all so concerned with Nick on third and John at the plate that I was becoming an afterthought. Honestly having to deal with those two guys was a handful, there wasn't much they could do about me anyway.

The pitcher stepped off and threw to third, but Nick was back in plenty of time to beat the throw. I jogged back to first, stood on the bag and waited for everyone to get set again so I could take a lead. That's when Pete leaned over to me and whispered, "When you take your lead, just keep going. Don't wait for the pitch, let's see what happens."

Sure, why not? I said to myself, half sarcastically and half hysterically. I had seen Tricky Nick do this before, so I knew it was possible. If I could get close enough to the second baseman (all I needed was a good step on him) there was no way he or the shortstop would be able to cover a throw if they even made one. This wasn't an unusual situation, and lots of times they would just concede the stolen base rather than giving the runner on third a chance to get home. Nick was way too dangerous so they probably wouldn't even risk it, but I had a feeling they might. The Southside team was coached by Travis who was well known for his aggressive gameplay, they might even go for a double pickoff. My heart started beating harder and I wiped my hands down the front of my uniform. Watching Nick do it was one thing but experiencing it myself was something else. I was determined though, and also determined not to mess it up in front of all these people.

John stepped into the batter's box. The pitcher went into the stretch and Nick took a big lead down third. No one was looking at me, so I just walked out ...one step......two steps.... three steps...

I was past the first baseman but he was playing up so I was behind him. If he could see me in his peripheral vison, he didn't seem to care what I was doing, he was watching on John and Nick. The second baseman was pretty much dead center between first and second base, a little "up" but not enough for me to get behind him. I was trying to keep casual, but the adrenaline was starting to get the best of me.

Another step...five-step leads were big but not unheard of ....

The pitcher hadn't even looked over at me, he was totally focused on Nick.

Another step...I was getting pretty close to the second baseman, who was starting to look over at me...

...and that's when I couldn't keep it together anymore and just took off.

Keep in mind, the pitcher still had the ball. And a very difficult decision he had to make, fast.

I dove for the base as soon as I was close enough. Our coaches told us over and over that sliding was better than diving when stealing a base, and we shouldn't dive because it slowed you down and was more dangerous. I couldn't help it; it was like I was almost to the boat out in deep water and just lunged for safety.

In. Safe. No throw.

So, one out, Tricky Nick on third, me on second, power hitting John up and we are about to manufacture a run with one of the gnarliest plays known to baseball. Why not? The worst that could happen was pretty much everything. But there was also a chance that it would work. It felt like the odds were about even from where

I was.

We all looked over to Coach Wilson at third for the sign. He tapped his right bicep twice, for bunt. Here we go. Not even waiting on another pitch or two. Pete liked to keep the pressure on once he felt like he had an advantage, and that's what he was doing here.

The pitcher went into the stretch, and Nick took a standard three-step lead down the third base line. No shenanigans from anyone this time, he wound up and threw. John squared up the bunt and laid it down. It was excellent, trickled down the first base line and stopped rolling about twelve feet from the plate, staying fair. The infield was completely surprised. John took off for first, and now it was a race between Nick and the pitcher. He might have a play at the plate if he could get to the ball and if Nick didn't get a good jump.

From my vantage point halfway between second and third, it looked like it was going to be close. Nick hadn't taken a very big lead prior to the pitch, and he only shuffled an extra step during the windup so he wasn't as far off the bag as any of us would have preferred, but this was Tricky Nick, he could go from standing still to all out sprint in an instant, which is what happened here. He blew the doors out getting home, continuing to accelerate and reaching the plate at the same time the pitcher reached the ball. The catcher was pointing to first base, letting the pitcher know that was where the only play was. He made a really great throw after fielding the ball barehanded and got the force at first before John could get there, but the damage was already done. Nick was in safe. Tie game.

In all the action I had advanced to third, leaving me as the go ahead run on third with two outs. That's where

I would stay though. Matty drew a walk, and the next kid was hit by a pitch, so we had bases loaded. The next batter took the second pitch deep to center, and it looked good off the bat, but the centerfielder made a nice running catch for out number three. I was left stranded on third, and the score remained tied at 5-5.

As I was grabbing my glove in the dugout I asked Ricky, "Is the All-Star game always like this?"

"Any game Pete is coaching against Travis ends up like this, remember?"

Travis and Pete were good friends and they loved competing with each other, kinda like me and Ricky. When I was on Pete's team and we played Travis' team, I guess it did tend to get a little out of hand now that I remembered it, but in a fun way. These two clearly did not like to lose to each other.

The next inning was both stressful and uneventful at the same time for both sides. The coaches were making strategic shifts and substitutions, bullpens were getting empty, but the score remained tied up at 5-5 going into the seventh, the last inning of the game.

THE SEVENTH INNING

Because of all the lineup changes and strategic coaching movements I was now playing second base. I didn't play a lot of infield. Not that it was a big deal, and usually second base was fairly straight forward but this situation was going to be different. My friend Paulie was going to be trying to close it out, and he was a left-handed pitcher. Things were most likely going to be coming to my side of the field if hitters could connect, especially if they started to empty the bench and send in all the lefty hitters they had. I was pretty sure that wouldn't matter too much though. Paulie had an edge that only a handful of people knew about. He could throw a real curve ball.

Curve balls look weird and act weird. They are slower, probably the slowest breaking pitch a pitcher will throw. If you watch the pros, you'll see that curve balls have almost a wave action happening, like a looping drop. Most pitchers have what's called the 12-to-6 curve, meaning the ball is going to drop down, from the 12 o'clock position to the 6 o'clock position, and this happens right in front of the plate.

There are variations to curves, too. You can have it curve and drop to the pitcher's glove hand side. Sometimes pitchers will have it start high, looking like a high outside pitch but then at the last second it will drop into the zone for a strike. The real nasty ones actually have a "hill riding" effect, like the ball is going up a little hill then drops way back down the backside. I've never understood the physics behind how these pitches work, and trying to hit something like that, especially at our age and steady diet of four-seam fastballs was no easy feat.

I knew other kids who claimed they could throw curves, and there was some movement on them for sure. Throwing any kind of breaking pitch is difficult, and throwing one that doesn't either get demolished into another dimension by the batter or end up behind the catcher is challenging. Most of the ones I had seen outside of Paulie's did move enough to be called a curve ball, but they weren't anything to be afraid of. Also, most pitchers had different grips and release points that made it easy to tell when it was coming.

Paulie's curve was a true hill rider. It had a little bump up and then the bottom would drop out, and he threw it with almost the exact same motion and release that all his other pitches had. It was evil, like somehow he had switched out the hardball with a wiffle ball.

The only issue would be when to tip his hand. Once he threw one the element of surprise would be gone because it was so obvious. We had an infielders meeting on the mound before the inning started, and Coach Pete basically said, "Use it when you need it but try not to need it," which is how it went for the first two batters. Paulie was really good and had spot-on location with his fastball today. But their last guy, their last hope, potential out number three or go-ahead run, was a real piece of work. He made contact on everything, was a real good defensive hitter, fouling off several fastballs. Finally, Matty the catcher put down the number two, curve ball.

It was a textbook curve that Paulie delivered, too. That thing started out about numbers high and dropped down to knee high about three feet in front of the plate, swing and a miss. The entire infield was holding our breath and trying to look casual.

There was some chattering in their dugout. They had noticed, but it didn't matter. Paulie didn't even need to throw another curve, the kid at bat was so confused he couldn't really get his "batters' eye" back so that was it. Two more pitches and he was out on strikes. We had last bats and a chance to win.

I was up second so took my spot in the on-deck circle and started practice swings. I was facing the crowd, looking at the stands just taking easy swings getting loose when I heard a strange whizzing/hissing sound. That's when I knew who was closing for Southside. Mike Dobbs.

Like I said, I knew Mike, went to school with him. He was a big quiet kid, which made him even scarier. He showed no emotion, like a shark. I could hear his pitches whizzing by from the on-deck circle, and I knew that they would be sizzling when I got in the batter's box.

Tricky Nick was up in front of me, and he was out in four pitches, walking back to the dugout looking flustered. One out.

I went through my usual routine and looked down at Coach Wilson for the sign. "Swing away," green light. I stepped into the box, tapped the opposite corner of the plate to square myself and got ready. Mike went into his windup and let one rip, right at me. I hit the dirt and heard it hit the backstop from my spot on the ground with a bang. Our whole dugout booed, "C'mon ump, that was on purpose!" but it didn't matter to me. I took it as a sign of respect, but at the same time I wasn't going to let him mess around with me. Besides, if I got hit, and survived, it meant I was on base, the winning run.

This time I tapped the opposite corner of the plate and really crowded it, about as close as I could get without being on it. We were testing each other a bit here, and I thought I saw something in his eyes before the pitch, maybe a flicker, but I couldn't be sure, it was over in an instant and then the ball was coming.

This pitch was down in the dirt, near enough to my feet that I knew what he was saying. He was having fun, but I wasn't going to back off. We were just two guys who knew each other going at it, like Pete and Travis. Now the count was 2-0. He was going to have to throw a strike. I was ready.

This time stepping in there was no funny stuff, no

strategic positioning. We both knew it was going to be in the zone, just a matter of whether he could throw it hard enough to get it past me. And let me say, he really tried. That pitch sounded like it should have had sparks coming out the back.

I think he was trying to keep it up in the zone, most hitters have a tough time catching up to those when they have a typical power-arcing swing style. My style wasn't power, it was contact and hustle, and that's what I did. I just barely caught it with the end of the bat, but it was enough. The ball went through the gap between the shortstop and second base, into centerfield, base hit. I was on, the winning run on first base. One out. My hands were stinging from the contact.

I was no Tricky Nick, but I could move. I knew I was going to have to steal second to eliminate the double play potential, and I knew that Mike had seen me steal a base in the fifth inning, so he was going to be ready for it.

"Having fun? I'm having fun. This is a great game, isn't it? Man, what a game. All comes down to this."

What?

It was Pete. Still coaching first base. He was looking at the batter but talking to me. I began to wonder if being out there in the sun all afternoon plus the stress of the game had finally gotten to him. I was on first base. There was one out and the guy on the mound was probably the hardest throwing kid in the league. I wasn't even sure I was going to get to second base but OK, I guess?

I looked over at Coach Wilson on third for the sign. Take, hold the bag, no steal. I stepped out to a decent three-step lead as Mike went into the stretch, watching me over his shoulder. The first basemen, Kurt Schneider, who was a total a-hole and wannabe-tough-guy, said "Take another step, jerkwad."

I couldn't help it, I laughed. Mike stepped off the mound, so I jogged back. Of course, Kurt said "What's so funny? Huh? You got something to say?" I did not have something to say, but I made sure to step on his foot with my cleats as I walked off the bag taking my lead. I had played against Kurt enough to know that pain and humiliation were the only ways to get through to him. Words were pointless. He wasn't intimidating at all, and I suspected he was only there because his dad owned the insurance agency that was a team sponsor. I could think of several guys off the top of my head on his team who were better than him.

Mike went into the stretch again, staring me down over his shoulder, again. I figured even if I wasn't Tricky Nick, I could be enough like him to cause enough of a distraction to maybe get them to focus on me more than the hitter. We were still on "take, no steal" but they didn't know that. This time I took a bigger lead, got into a wide stance, and shook my hands a little bit, trying to bait them into throwing.

No deal. Mike delivered a screaming fastball for strike one.

"How you feeling Peaches?"

Uh … what? Pete was chatting while I was standing there on first. "Good?"

"Good. This is fun, isn't it? I love it. Love it. Let's keep having fun, ok?"

Dude was going over the edge out here. "OK."

I looked over at third base for the sign. Coach Wilson wiped down both forearms and swung. Steal.

Here we go.

One thing about big guys who are pitchers is that they usually aren't real quick. Their windups are like a demonstration of converting inertia into energy and Mike was no exception. I knew he probably had an OK pickoff move, but as long as he didn't catch me too far off the bag I wasn't worried. I also knew that once he started his windup I had a good chance to steal because it was going to take a bit for him to get the ball out of his hand. That was my window. All I had to do was time it right, and that meant I had to commit to running once I thought he was going to throw.

He went into the stretch, and I took a regular three-step lead. He started at me over his shoulder for what felt like two full minutes but was probably like four seconds. I wasn't leaning or wiggling my hands or really doing anything to tip off that I was going to run, but everyone knew this was a steal situation so there was a higher level of awareness than usual.

Mike turned and started his windup, and I took off. It was all a matter of execution now. I wasn't looking at anything other than second base. I could hear my heart beating in my ears and the crunch of the infield dirt under my cleats. Please don't let me screw this up in front of all these people. *Please.*

Five more steps. Four more. From third base I heard Coach Wilson yelling "Down, down, down!" but it didn't matter, I knew I was going to be sliding the moment I started running.

Two more steps. The second baseman was at the bag now, covering with his glove up. The throw was coming.

One more step.... down for the slide...hooked my

foot to catch the outside edge of the base and avoid the infielder's foot that was blocking the lead edge.

I felt the base and then the tag. I just laid there, not moving. Second baseman was holding the tag on my hip.

"Safe! The runner is safe!" yelled the ump. I put my hand up, signaling for a time out so I could get up. That was close. I stood up, dusted the dirt off my pants and looked over at Coach Wilson, who was clapping "Good job Peaches! Good hustle, good hustle. Keep your head on out there!"

The dugout was getting a little rowdy as well. Some guys had rally hats on, and they were tapping aluminum bats on the top of the fence clanging away. The pitch Mike had thrown was a strike, and it was time for him to get back to work.

Now that I was on second, I had to be more careful. Mike didn't have me behind him anymore, I was now just a glance over his right shoulder, and in his peripheral vision all the time. Even though he didn't have a gnarly pickoff move, it was still dangerous to mess around out there.

Coach Wilson gave the sign. Green light, swing away, so I took a lead as he went into the stretch, just an easy few steps out. I checked where the shortstop and centerfielder were in case they were cheating in towards second trying for a pickoff, but they held their positions behind me.

Mike wound up and threw, and the batter, didn't know the kid before today, I think his name was Ryan, took a defensive swing and fouled it off towards the first base side. Way late getting around on it, but he was starting to get there. However, the count was now 0-2, and we all knew something nasty was coming.

Mike went into the stretch and didn't really pay me much attention this time, all business on this pitch. It was a heater, I could hear it whizzing from out on second base, but it was right down the center of the plate.

Ryan got to it this time, barely. It was on the ground and headed towards the first base side, fair ball, a hard spinning grounder. When the second baseman moved, I moved too, taking off for third. He didn't field it cleanly; it took a bit of an awkward double hop so he had no time for a throw to third. The only play was the force at first, which he got.

Two out. Me, the winning run, on third base. Bottom of the seventh. Because it was an exhibition game, there would be no extra innings, so if we didn't score the game would end in a tie, which none of us wanted. Even if we could have kept going, I'm pretty sure both teams were about out of pitchers at this point anyway.

I wasn't real familiar with the next batter either, some kid named Tom, went to St. Giles, also didn't know him before today. We looked down for the sign, and it was "swing away." Why not at this point, it probably didn't matter. I was starting to feel like there were quite a lot of things out of my control right now while I was standing there, once again finding myself having deep questions on third base.

It also occurred to me that this was the first time Mike and I had ever been in this kind of pressure situation together. We were classmates, had been since first grade. We had played kickball and dodgeball and stuff against each other in gym class plenty of times. This was a different. He was looking right at me now, in the stretch. I took a three-step lead but had no plans for going anywhere unless the batter made contact.

Mike wound up and threw. This one bounced in the dirt in front of the plate and went behind the catcher, but Tom still swung for strike one. He was way behind, and seemed kinda scared, or maybe it was the pressure of the situation we were in. I doubted he would be able to catch up on any of the next pitches, it looked like he was having a hard time getting comfortable in there.

The catcher jogged the ball back out to the mound, and the infield all came in for a quick meeting. As I walked back to third base Coach Wilson and Coach Pete traded signs, but it was fast, and I couldn't figure it all out. Coach Wilson quietly said, "You gotta run man."

He wasn't even looking at me, so I wasn't sure if this was direction or what. It was like he was making an observation.

"Ok coach, if he can make contact I'm gone, I can get there." We were in bad shape if we were hoping this kid can get a hit, I thought, but you have to play the hand you're dealt I guess.

"That's not what I'm talking about." Coach Wilson was looking across at Pete, still talking to me but not looking at me. "We can't wait and see if we can hit this guy. You barely did, and I don't think anyone left coming up is going to have a chance if we even get past Tommy, which it doesn't look like is going to happen. You gotta go on the pitch."

Comprehension, clarity and fear all hit me at the same time. They wanted me to steal home *on the windup*. This is insane. This is INSANE. My heart was instantly pounding in my chest, and my left leg started shaking so badly I couldn't put weight on it for a few seconds. I had to bend down and re-tie my shoe to try and get a handle on myself. This was crazy.

The concept was simple enough. The pitcher's windup is slow enough that if I time it right he won't be able to get the ball to the plate before I get there, and if he deviates from his throwing motion it's a balk and I get the base free. That is the theory anyway. While not many have tested this theory, from what I have seen I can say that it's about twenty percent true. Meaning twenty percent successful. Optimistically.

I had never been here before. I was usually watching someone else, usually Ricky, make the big game-winning play. It was all on the line, and it was all coming down to … me. I didn't have a lot of time to think about it though, and that was a good thing. "Are you guys sure about this?" I asked. I needed to hear something reassuring because I was not sure about this at all.

"There're no better options my man, and believe me, we've tried to think of one."

"Thanks Coach. I feel a lot better now."

"Just go when I say go and get down when I say get down."

Infield meeting was over, and I looked over at Pete coaching first. He wiped down both forearms and swung an imaginary bat. Steal.

I was trying to act casual, but it was difficult because I was totally wired. It felt like there was a lightning storm happening in my head. Tom stepped in and Mike went into the stretch. I took a generous (but not *too* generous) lead down the third base line, and twisted my left foot a bit, trying to dig in and get something extra to push off.

For a moment we all just stood there looking at each other. Me and Mike looking at each other across the infield, Tom and the catcher behind the plate looking at Mike. The crowd noise had faded into a murmur. I noticed the banners by the concession stand fluttering in the breeze.

Mike looked down, and then leaned back, signaling the start of his windup and Coach Wilson whisper yelled "*GO!*" from behind me.

The first few steps I took felt like the atmosphere had somehow become incredibly dense and I was trying to run through a thick fog. Everything was slow and muffled around me. I could hear and feel the thud of each step I took. My legs felt heavy and disconnected. *That's it,* I thought, *no way I can get there like this.*

It was over in a blink. All of a sudden everything came rushing back and I was in real-time hauling ass down the third base line. Tom still had his back to me, waiting for the pitch. The catcher saw I was coming so he was starting to get up out of his squat as much as possible in order to block the plate and make the tag when he got the ball. I don't know what Mike was doing on the mound, hopefully still pitching, but no time to find out, I was digging as hard as I could and listening for Coach Wilson, trusting him to tell me when to slide.

It felt like it took forever. It wasn't that far from third base to home, but it seemed to me like I had been taking a lot of strides and then I heard Coach Wilson's voice booming "DOWN! DOWN NOW DOWN NOW!" so I went into a slide.

Tom had stepped back and to the rear side of the play, out of the way by now, and before I turned over to stretch the slide I could see him screaming and pointing down at the ground and then I was sliding.

Felt the plate under my right toe and then I hear the

"whap" of the ball hit the catcher's glove and felt the tag on my leg.

"Safe!" Yelled the ump.

"PEACHES ARE YOU EFFING KIDDING ME," Ricky yelled as he jumped the dugout fence and ran out, everyone charging out after him. Tom had already helped me up and then he tackled me and everyone else just piled on.

Everyone was freaking out. The stands were just roaring; at least that's what my dad told me later. I couldn't hear anything underneath the pile of kids who were on me. My family and some of the neighbors who were at the game were all super impressed that my teammates carried me off the field, but it was more because I was hyperventilating than anything else. Eventually they put me back down so we could line up and shake hands.

Mike was at the end of the handshake line, last kid before the coaches. I couldn't see his face so I couldn't tell if he was upset or what. I didn't know what to say. "Good game" seemed a little empty in this situation. All the other guys in line were cool, high-five's and "good game man, nice play" or something like that. After all, it was just an exhibition, it didn't count for anything other than bragging rights.

However, it was a baseball game, and someone had to lose (or I suppose we all would have lost if it had ended in a tie, but it didn't so that was beside the point now). I was hoping he wasn't upset because I liked Mike, he was my friend, we had known each other a long time. I didn't want him to think it was personal, like that pitcher from Gilchrest Hardware who I guess hated me now. It was just part of the game and it happened to work out that it was me and him, that's all. Plus, he was a big dude, and I made it a personal policy long ago to try not to make big dudes angry at me.

When I got to him, he was grinning and shaking his head, more bemused than upset. He didn't high five me, he actually stopped and shook my hand, "What the hell, man. First time in the All-Star game, and you go and do that? That was crazy. *You're* crazy. Good game. Also, don't try it on me again, that was your one time," and he poked his finger into my chest, still grinning.

I was so relieved. He had been the hero so many times it was nice that he understood the situation, and he was completely cool. I said, "I've never seen anyone throw like you man, seriously. We couldn't get a hit; we had nothing else left to try. Great game." I gave him that one armed, three pats on the back coach hug, and then a playful fist tap into his chest, which was not typical for us, but it felt right. Mike returned it, smiling.

Pete and Travis, the coaches, had reached each other.

"I guess I owe you dinner," Travis said to Pete as they shook hands. They were both grinning like idiots at each other, like me and Mike.

"Yeah, but I'll buy the first round, that was pretty close. Too close, I thought for a second Peaches wasn't going to get there."

I looked over at Mike and said," He's right, I thought I was out for sure."

Coach Wilson, from behind Pete, said "Me too, your slow ass took so long to get in gear I thought the lights were going to come on before you got home."

I couldn't even be mad if I wanted to. We were all standing around the infield talking, back patting, giving each other high fives, and talking smack. All kinds of people were coming up to me from out of the stands, patting me on the back, on the head, on the glove. It was … cool. Nothing like that had ever happened to me before, and I had no way of knowing at the time that it would be many years before I experienced something close to it again. Some people never do.

10
FOURTH OF JULY: EARLY EVENING

After dinner on the Fourth of July is a combination of excitement, unease, and impatience. Most of us were hanging around talking, just waiting for it to get dark, which was occurring with a maddening sort of leisure. I was still wearing my baseball uniform, hadn't really had a chance to change after the game and the dinner/party and then family and neighbors and stuff. Everyone who hadn't been there had heard about the game and I guess it just felt right to leave the uniform on while telling people things like "It was a team effort, great group of guys to be out there with," pretending I was answering sportswriters post-game interview questions. It was fun being "the guy" for once. Usually it was Ricky, but even he was having a good time being my hype man and seemed to enjoy me being in the spotlight for once, "No no no … that's not it at all, I saw the whole thing from the dugout, let me tell you what really happened…"

I was out front with Ant, drinking fruit punch from a plastic cup and talking. There was a streetlight in front of his house, and we were discussing our unsuccessful efforts to shoot it out. I have a lot of respect for whoever engineered those lights, because we had thrown (literally in some instances) everything we could think of at it, and it shrugged off each assault without any issue. It was so frustrating.

Ant's house had a porch that ran across the front, and there was no front railing or anything there. His dad was sitting out there in a folding lawn chair with a cigar, a beer, and a cooler next to him. Mr. Kaminski was a pretty calm guy. He had five kids, ran his own successful trucking company, was one of those big but gentle types who had seen it all and just did what he wanted without much worry about perceptions or consequences.

We all liked him, and I think he liked us too. He would help us build ramps to jump our bikes off exactly how we asked, never concerned with it being "too high" or "too steep" or "totally unsafe." He enjoyed watching us try to take those ramps on and fail catastrophically. He'd just sit on his porch with a smirking laugh and yell "Shake it off, you almost had it" or "Just rub some dirt on it and get going, you'll be fine" because I think he wanted to see us keep going, trying to land stupider and stupider stuff. I suspect that if he was younger he probably would have been right out there with us.

I remember looking up at the streetlight, which had just turned on, and seeing something flying at us out of my peripheral vison. It seemed about the size of Mr. Kaminski's cigar butt. I thought he had tossed it at us for whatever reason.

There was a flash, like instant daylight. Then it felt

like all the air was sucked back and away from us, and then it all came rushing back at once with a massive BOOM and heat and then I couldn't hear anything.

I can now speak with some authority when I say that what you see in movies and on TV about explosions is mostly wrong. There's a flash and stuff goes up in the air, they get that part right. But until you have actually been near a decent sized explosion you just don't understand all the forces in play and the effects they can have on a person.

Everything seemed far away. Ant, the streetlight, it all seemed like I was in a memory of something that had already happened that was still happening, and I was just remembering it while it was going on. Complete tunnel vison. Everything gray. Very far away I could hear someone screaming. My hearing and vision came rushing back in an extended high-pitched whine. The colors refocused. My ears were ringing but I realized the screaming was Ant, still standing right next to me. He was screaming, "*What did you do that for you could have killed us are you crazy?*"

James Barlow had thrown an M-1000, which is equivalent to a quarter stick of dynamite, from the side of his house, over the Kaminski's porch, and it had landed about three feet behind us on the sidewalk. We knew exactly where it landed because there was a singed dimple on the concrete there now. I didn't get hit by any debris, I don't think Ant did either and we still aren't sure how. We should have. Ant was super mad, screaming, pointing at the side of the house, pointing at the crater, pointing at me. I still couldn't really hear well, basically in a daze shaking my head and rubbing my eyes.

I don't know if it was the force of the blast or my reaction, but I had fruit punch all over the front of my uniform and I wasn't holding the cup anymore. I don't remember what happened to it. Mr. Kaminski was still sitting there on the porch watching, apparently unfazed. He seemed to have no idea what had actually happened and thought this was all good fun, neighborhood kids playing on the Fourth of July stuff. I was still in shock for the most part. It was the closest I'd ever been to an explosion that powerful, and it was scary. I had felt that blast, the heat, an actual shockwave, the pressure drop in my ears, all of it.

I was so mad at James. I think that moment was the maddest I'd ever been at *anyone* up to that point. My All-Star uniform was probably ruined, I had nearly been blown up and this dude just kept getting away with it. I didn't care anymore, I wanted to get him back right the hell now. I considered going to get my bat and going looking of him, but even as mad as I was, I knew that would be a bad idea. We already had something ready to go, now I was just hoping he would be in there when it went off, and hopefully it went off on him.

Also, I really wanted to know where the hell was James getting this stuff. The bigger the explosion generally meant the more expensive the firework, and this one plus the stuff him and his buddies had chucked at us when we were playing Hotbox equaled a good chunk of change. I knew he didn't have a job. Where was it coming from, and more importantly, how much more did he have? I was contemplating that when:

zzzzzzzZZZZIP BANG, a bottle rocket blew behind us.

"Haha hey ... hey good one!" yelled a voice from

above.

The Smedleys were still on the roof, still at it. I had forgotten about them to be honest. There was so much else going on that the occasional sniped bottle rocket just became part of the mix. I began to wonder just how many bottle rockets they had. They had been up there all day, and now it was starting to get dark, and they weren't letting up at all.

I went to sit on my front porch to regroup and regain my senses. My relatives had all headed home or to fireworks shows (the professional kind) and I knew my folks were going to be heading to the high school soon to see our local show, which was always pretty good. I usually attended with them and my brother, but that wasn't the plan this year.

"We're leaving in 10 minutes" my mom yelled out the front window.

My brother, wearing his lucky number seven jersey and dirty knees, came trotting down Hoffman's driveway from the alley where he and Andy had been throwing ladyfingers at each other. Ladyfingers were mini firecrackers, although they had regular sized fuses on them which made them look even more ridiculous. They were mostly harmless if you could say that about any firework, but you could hold one of these in your hand when it went off and all you would feel is a little heat. No big deal.

"Did you hear that one earlier? I saw the flash first, that was big."

"Yeah, I was standing next to it, somehow James Barlow has more quarter sticks, watch out over there."

"Oh. Yeah ok. You coming with?" Meaning to the fireworks show at the high school. I was not. Ricky and

I had to set up the rocket/stink bomb launchpad to Barlow's garage window and this would be the perfect time. Most people headed to the show, it was only like eight blocks to the high school, very walkable. If you didn't want to go sit in the grandstands (and wanted to keep drinking, which most of the adults wanted to by now and drinking was not allowed in the stadium) there was an empty lot on the other side of the "L" tracks where people would bring lawn chairs and blankets and sit out and watch the show in a more relaxed and lubricated environment. All you missed from over there was the ground displays, which were ok, but the main show was up in the air anyway so no big loss.

"Nah, I'm a little tired from the game, and the bomb that a-hole threw at me and Ant kinda gave me a headache, I'm going to take it easy here for a bit and catch up with you guys later in the field." This was total fabrication, and my brother probably knew it was total fabrication, but now he had plausible deniability *and* he could verify my story and whereabouts. Not the first time for us with this type of situation.

"OK, see you later."

"Yah have fun."

My mom stopped by the front porch on their way out to offer her usual "Are you sure? Well, we're going to miss you, everyone is going to be asking where you are, you should go" speech, which every mom has to make prior to leaving one of the family behind no matter the importance of the event. She also told me to go soak my jersey in a bucket of cold water, "I might be able to get that stain out, but don't get your hopes up." Crap.

They left, I grabbed a soda from the fridge and went

into my room to change out of my fruit punch-stained uniform. I had zero remorse for what we were about to do to the garage. Honestly, now I hoped it burned down somehow, with him in it. I sat there for a minute envisioning that – the fire trucks, the fire – and thinking about the satisfaction I assumed would come with it. I was still angry about my jersey and almost getting killed and everything else this jerk had done. Let's get on with it.

I had a set of camos that I got from the Army-Navy Surplus store on Madison Street, but I decided not to wear them. Way too suspicious – I might as well have put on an orange shirt that said "Definitely Up To Something" on the front. None of the other kids were wearing pants, let alone military style fatigues, and I wanted to blend in, even though the camo would have been useful for the staging portion of the operation.

I ended up with my Van Halen shirt because it was mostly black, and green shorts with the deep hip pockets, figuring that was camoflauge-ish but not too conspicuous. This time I went out the back door and hopped the fence into Ricky's yard, then around the side and up to the deck doors. Payback time was about to begin.

Our plan was to get everything set up under Ricky's deck while folks were out watching the big show. Even if you didn't walk over to the stadium you could still see some of the big ones from the street out front, and the remaining neighbors who hadn't gone were out there now, so it would be the perfect cover for us. Once that show was over people would filter back and then the actual fun stuff would start, and that was when we would light the candle and then head over to the field.

All those boxes and bags and pocketsful of fireworks people had been saving were going to be lit off, primarily in Emerson field but some people (Mr. Kaminski) would just chuck them in the front or wherever. They didn't have to worry about the cops like we did, but the field was great for that. You could see all sides so they couldn't sneak up easily, and there were plenty of different directions and yards you could run to (or through) if you needed to shake the law.

I could see through the deck doors. Ricky was sitting at one end of the couch playing Missile Command on Atari. I tapped the glass and let myself in.

"Hey Peaches. New high score almost, let me finish this game."

"Yup."

"Did you bring it?"

"Yup."

"It" was a tapered candle, like the kind you would put in a dining room table candleholder or something. Fancy, but apparently not fancy enough (or perhaps too fancy) for my mom because it had been unused for years in the drawer of the hutch thing in our dining room among some cloth napkins and napkin rings (Seriously, who used those? We had like three sets that never left the draw my entire life). Years later my mom confessed to me that she was actually afraid of lit candles which was why we had so many unused tapers and Christmas candles and tea lights. I guess when she was little there was a fire in her neighborhood and the cause was an unattended candle. She had latched on to the "candle" part of the story and disregarded the "unattended" part, so we never had lit candles in the house, except on a cake for your birthday.

We were all out of birthday candles now, not because there had been a lot of celebrating happening, but because Ricky and I had burned through them all making booby traps and experimenting. The conclusion we arrived at, definitively after using the time elapse feature of my Timex, was that there was no way a birthday candle would give us the length of delay we needed to pull this off. We needed to get this set up and be over in Emerson field well before anything launched, and really the longer we could delay it the better. The more demolitions mayhem that was happening in and around the neighborhood, the greater chance no one would notice this thing going off.

The simple solution was a bigger candle. We learned that one of those tapers could burn for a long time, and it was still comparatively small enough that we could keep it concealed and shielded from the wind with our set up. Even better, the candle I had was black (no idea how *that* ended up in our house) so we were in a good spot there.

Ricky missed the high score, so we headed outside to our spot under the deck to get set up. We had:

One 1/4 oz. rocket

One Black Cat bottle rocket

One stink bomb

One 1/16 oz. cone-shaped lead slip sinker

One roll of clear tape

One tapered candle, black

One ball of modelling clay, green

We had stashed a small piece of aluminum gutter under the deck, a two-foot section that we had found in the alley, figuring it would be a good launch chute. It was still under there, along with a few landscape pavers and a couple unused large terra cotta pots we had gathered.

Tapers burn slow, so we decided to cut this one down instead of trying to bury most of it, and using the modeling clay for positioning was a lot easier than dirt. They also burn a lot brighter than birthday candles, so we had to position the terra cotta pots just right or anyone walking down the alley would see the soft glow of candlelight coming from underneath the Hoffmans' deck. There was a breeze, but it wasn't much so we felt wind would not be a factor, which was good for both keeping the candle lit as well as targeting and trajectory.

"OK, so keep this side of it shielded. What are you doing?"

"A little extra special something on there, payback for that quarter stick." I was taping a Jumping Jack on to our rocket.

"Why did we go through all this stuff if you are going to just burn the garage down anyway? You know that it's full of wood and cardboard right?"

"I don't care. He could have killed me and Ant, and I hope he's nearby or even better in there when this goes off."

"*Dude.*"

"What? What would you do?"

"I think the stink bomb is enough, c'mon now Peaches. Take that thing off there and let's stick to the plan."

"Screw you man, I want to burn it down."

"Listen to you! I know you're mad, and I want to get even too but we can't just start torching stuff, at least not yet anyway. Besides, I want to see what happens, and if you burn the garage down we'll never know."

He had a point there. Reluctantly I un-taped the Jumping Jack and put it back in my pocket. "Sorry."

"Nah, don't be. You're mad for a good reason. He'll get what's coming to him, but let's try and stay out of jail, ok?"

"Yeah, ok. Let's get this set up and get out of here."

Three minutes later and it was done. We were going to stop back and light the candle right before we headed over to the field later. We checked to make sure the coast was clear and headed back out front where we could hear the action starting to heat up.

11
FOURTH OF JULY: NIGHTTIME

Now that it was dark, people were starting to get into the true spirit of the holiday. I could hear the show at the high school kicking off. They always set off a couple of the big boomers first just to make sure everyone was paying attention. Down the block there were sparklers lighting up and a few people had jumping jacks they were setting off. All flash, no boom. Kids' stuff.

The largest boom so far was coming the Smedleys' roof. You could tell by looking down the block where the action was. There were groups of people out watching the high school show from the street, or just hanging out chatting, some folks still had lawn chairs out there. Not in front of the Smedleys' place though, that was a live fire zone that was littered with red bottle rocket sticks already, and no one wanted to test their luck.

I have no idea how they kept it up, but they were still

shooting off rockets, and the intensity and frequency of their fire was starting to pick up. Up until now it had been kinda random, and they weren't really shooting off anything big, once in a while sending a whistler down the street but for the most part just standard bottle rockets, which explode with less force than a regular firecracker. It seems they had been saving the larger stuff for when it got dark, which was now, and they were starting to send it. It is also worth noting that they apparently had an inexhaustible supply of beer, because they had been drinking all day and weren't slowing down on that either.

Ricky and I had a couple packs of firecrackers we were lighting off one at a time at the end of his driveway near the street. Just goofing around, really. We were saving most of our stash for later when everyone went over to Emerson. It drew the Smedleys' attention because they began to focus their fire towards us. Ricky started taunting them:

"Haha you can't hit jack, have another beer."

"What was that? Did you get that from the toy store? In the safe for kids aisle? Maybe your mom picked them up for you, it's ok."

"Missssssssssss and a misssssss and a misssssssssss……………"

I'm not sure if they even heard him clearly, although he was yelling it at them, but it certainly seemed to intensify their rate of fire. Ricky was laughing and said to me, "So, think we should start shooting back?"

It was a good question. I don't think we had as much ammo as they did, but we were pretty well set up. What Hansen lacked in variety he made up for in quantity and passed the discount on to his customers. We still had more than half a gross of bottle rockets and probably about the same amount of firecrackers, plus some other assorted m-80s, and a couple of mortar and shell combos, but we weren't about to dip into the heavy expensive stuff for these knuckleheads.

"Yeah man, those guys have been up there all day, it's time they got a taste of their own medicine. I'll grab the pipes." We had specially cut pieces of conduit ready to go in my garage. I hopped the fence, grabbed them and about five packs of bottle rockets and met Ricky back in front. He had a lighter and a pack of punks, which were things that looked like incense sticks but smelled worse. Their only purpose as far as we knew was for lighting fuses without getting your hand too close, plus they stayed lit, so you don't have to worry about wind or hot lighters.

We had to get a better angle. From Ricky's driveway we would have to shoot over my house and that was too tricky, plus if my dad found out I was shooting over our house he would have killed me. Across the street would give us a great line of fire but there was one big problem – cover.

There was none. About a year ago they had redone all the sewers and tore up the streets, and I guess as part of that process the trees on that side of the street had to be cut down, about halfway down the block. There were saplings growing now but they were useless for cover. No one was stupid enough to leave their car parked on the street on the Fourth of July so there was absolutely nothing out there. We were going to have to shoot and scoot.

"Shoot and scoot from in front of the Swensons' house?"

"Yep. You fire I'll reload. Let's go."

"Keep it covered up until we get across the street."

We jogged across the street trying to keep the pipes and stuff hidden from view. Once we got over, I put rockets in both pipes, lit a punk, touched it to the fuse of one and handed it to Ricky, then crouched down on his opposite side ready to light and hand him the next. The shot went high, over the roof, and blew over their backyard. I touched the punk to the fuse and handed Ricky the next rocket and he handed me the empty pipe back to reload. This one went low and bounced off the front of their house but blew while it was on the rebound. That one definitely got their attention.

"Hey! Hey, you I see you over there, you're gonna get it!" one of them slurred at us.

Ricky put the next one directly onto the roof – *bam* - and yelled "How do you like that? Huh? Oh, you want some more? Ok."

The element of surprise was gone, and they started shooting back at us. I was reloading and lighting as fast as I could, and we were moving down the block towards the end. We were going to be out in the intersection soon, so we had to start going *back* to stay in range, which was a little scary, but we had no choice. Our rockets probably couldn't make the shot from the next block but theirs could no doubt. Shoot and scoot, shoot and scoot.

It was starting to get intense. Both of them were now firing down at us, and one of them was shooting those No. 2 rockets that leave a trail and blow up in a shower of sparks. I had heard the tales of epic firework battles in the cemetery near the expressway and had always wondered what they were like. I did not expect to be having the experience in front of my house.

All our parents were still at the fireworks show at the high school, so there was no one around to put a stop to it. Even though the Smedleys were adults they sure as hell were not responsible and the only other adult who was out there that could have done something was Mr. Kaminski. He was never one to interrupt fun in the name of safety, so he was sitting on his front porch enjoying the scene unfolding, drinking a beer.

We traded fire for a little while. We must have scored a couple pretty close hits because twice they yelled and then threw full lit packs of firecrackers down at us. We were starting to get low on ammo and Ricky was going to make a run for it and also to grab a garbage can lid to use as a shield when we noticed someone walking down the middle of Pleasant Street, towards our block.

"Look at that! Wait…is that who I think it is? Holy shhh… it is!" It was Mrs. Vizzone. She was headed this way. And she was walking with purpose. The Smedleys must have seen her too because they immediately redirected their fire towards her.

Mrs. Vizzone (not Grandma "Ma" Vizzone, this was Tony's wife) was more of a phenomenon than a figure. Seldom seen unless there was something that they needed handled or settled, although more often heard than seen. She somehow managed to keep all the Vizzones fed, clothed, and at school/work/parole meetings as they needed. From what I understood from Stacy, the youngest, she was the final word in any disagreements, and while conversations could get heated, not one of them dared to push her too far. I suppose you had to develop into something like that when you were trying to bring order to that environment, but at the same time she must have had something to do with the creation of that environment in the first place, which was an equally impressive feat.

The other thing that made her unique was that we had never seen her leave the house. No one had. Sometimes she would pop out on the front porch, and the upper and lower back porches were connected in that Chicago two-flat style so she would go up and down back there, but we had never seen her out in the neighborhood, or anywhere else for that matter, until now. Ricky later told me he actually thought she had some kind of disability or health condition that kept her from walking more than a couple steps at a time. My mom thought she only had one leg and a prosthetic. Everyone had a theory.

By now folks who had stayed here and not gone to the fireworks show had noticed that there was another impromptu one happening at the end of the block and, naturally, were curious. I could see the Swensons, Keltons and Pavliks on their front porches watching. Some of the kids and their parents had wandered down towards this end of the block, stopping about halfway which was safely out of the live fire zone.

Everyone seemed to realize what was happening at the same time as Mrs. Vizzone rounded the corner onto our end of the block, under intensifying fire from the Smedleys, who just were not letting up at all. They were quick learners; they had already incorporated the one loader/one shooter strategy Ricky and I had been using against them and were successfully laying down those No. 2 rockets at a pretty respectable clip for two drunk guys on a roof.

The Smedleys' house was second from the corner, in

between our house and the Abbotts. Mrs. Vizzone got to the front of their house, still in the street, and said something up to the guys. We couldn't make it out, and apparently neither could they because Charlie yelled down, "What's that?" As he sent another rocket down whoooOOOOSH BANG

"I said, did you know that Stacy's in the circus?" Mrs. Vizzone replied.

This was starting to get very weird.

"No kidding? Hey that's great! Good for her, you must be proud." Whoosh BANG!

"Oh, we are. She's been taking tumbling classes at the college for years now."

"Really? Wow. She must be pretty good, it's not easy to get into the circus, right?

"Oh no, she had two auditions and there were a lot of other kids. She has to practice every day, even weekends!"

Whoosh BANG!

They were just having a normal conversation, but the guys never let up shooting at her. She never got hit, never even acknowledged that they were shooting at her, never flinched at an explosion.

"I just wanted to let you know, they will be performing next month at the convention center downtown."

"That's great! Thank you for letting us know, we'll have to try and make it. Tell Stacy we are proud of her too!" whooooOOOOSH BANG.

"OK well you have a good night."

"You too, happy Fourth of July!" And she turned and started walking, still in the middle of the street, back around the corner towards her house in a blaze of rocket fire. They guys never stopped shooting the whole time.

I looked at Ricky, shaking my head, "Did not expect that. I thought she was going to tell them to knock it off."

"I didn't even know she could walk that far."

This seemed like a good time to disengage from the Smedleys, so we headed back across the street to my front porch.

"We gotta light that candle and head over to the field."

"Yeah, let's go. I gotta get my stuff from the back, meet you there."

I headed down our driveway. I could hear the Smedleys overhead (now they were aiming straight up) while I grabbed my bag from under our back stairs where I had stashed it earlier. My mom did not approve of fireworks, but at the same time did not confiscate, only said "I don't want you having those in the house." My brother and I interpreted this as meaning we could have them *outside* of the house and therefore kept our stuff either tucked up in the boards under the back stairs or in the garage, but the garage was risky. That was my dad's domain, and he very much did approve of fireworks, and if he found them you knew it because he would set them off. I don't think he could help himself.

I was surprised when he came out the back door, saw me in the back yard with a bag and said "Heading over to the field? I'll join you, give me a minute to get your brother."

"OK, I'll wait here for you guys," shoot I couldn't get over to light that candle. My dad went back in the house, and I hissed over the fence, "Light it, don't wait for me."

From the darkness came "I know, I got it covered, meet you over there." Ricky had been hiding over there the whole time, so he knew I was compromised. It didn't matter, it was done and out of my hands regardless. Time to get the hell out of there. Besides, we had some good stuff to light now.

So did about half the neighborhood. It was pretty dark in the field itself, but I could make out a good twenty-ish people over there when we got there, including Pat Vizzone, Amy Barlow, Ant's brother Andy, Timbo, and some random adults like Al Swenson, Tom the Chef from down the block, I think one of the guys who lived in the apartments.

The air smelled like smoke and gunpowder and sulfur. There were a couple of smaller groups just lighting mostly small stuff, firecrackers and bottle rockets. There was a group in the middle of the field that was shooting up bigger stuff, primarily mortar-launched shells. It was pretty warm, but the breeze was starting to pick up, so the smoke was clearing a bit instead of hanging over the field like it did some years. I briefly hoped we had kept the ignition candle on our setup shielded enough but it was too late to do anything about it now, so I got back to matters at hand.

I had a paper grocery bag with about 74 bottle rockets, a lot of firecrackers, a few m80s, and the "special" we got from Pat Vizzone, my brother had a couple packs of lady fingers and firecrackers, and my dad had Silver Servers and I think m100s, or 1/8th sticks of dynamite. He told my mom he kept them around for when he went camping to "keep the bears away," which was not true, but it was good enough for her to dismiss them and that was that.

We got to work, mostly sending up bottle rockets and tossing firecrackers, but we ran out of the little stuff and moved to the bigger stuff. Seems like everyone else was running at the same pace we were because the number and intensity of things going up was steadily increasing. Someone busted out the roman candles, which I always enjoyed but could never afford.

Pat Vizzone was out in the middle of the field blasting mortars off, crouching down out there like an artillery gunner, except using a cigarette to light them. He had some good ones that went way up and changed colors or fizzled out waterfalls of white sparks. My dad and brother and I headed out there towards him to set off our best mortar – we had bought it from him, something called the Crazy Cracker. It was a shell that went up, popped a burst and then a tube of firecrackers on a parachute gently fell to earth while exploding sequentially. Allegedly. We had tried things like this before, most of the time the parachute either burns up and the shell drops like a rock or the chute opens fine but the shell doesn't ignite so it just floats to the ground like a big dud. This one was advertised to have overcome all the engineering challenges and was guaranteed to deploy effectively, so we had high hopes.

Pat lit off a whopper, it was so big that it would not have been out of place at the high school show. It went way up and blew into a beautiful green and white burst that looked as big as the field. He looked over to us and said, "You got one to light? Go ahead man," to my dad.

My dad set it down in the clearing in the grass, lit the fuse and jogged back a few steps so he was crouching next to Pat, I was down on his right and my brother was down on his left, forming a semicircle, all squatting or crouched down low in case it went off in the tube (which does happen enough to make you think about it). We were all intrigued by the Crazy Cracker, and its moment to shine had come.

When it went off, it didn't sound quite like the mortars Pat had been lighting. His had that "thump…whoosh" sequence, this had more of a "pop … whizz." It sounded wrong. The shell itself went up maybe sixteen feet, the burst happened, the parachute opened, and the firecrackers started going off, but it was way to low – at this point maybe ten feet off the ground - which was when the breeze really kicked up and changed the trajectory from straight down to over and down, onto my brother.

It didn't happen particularly fast. We could see what was happening and had enough time to react, it's just that none of us did, not even my brother. We all stood there and watched as a tube of exploding firecrackers gently floated down on to him. He tried to roll away at the last second, but it landed directly on him, and by rolling he actually tumbled up with it, all we could see was flashes of firecrackers and arms and legs and we could hear him yelling "Stop drop and roll," over and over again, apparently to himself, and that strategy was not working.

My dad and Pat got over to him first and managed to untangle the chute and get the thing off him and it went out. "You ok? You burned? Did you get hurt anywhere?" They were helping him up while patting him down making sure nothing was still burning on him. We couldn't see too well because it was pretty dark out there and the Crazy Cracker had temporarily flashed us, so I think we were all seeing spots too. My brother was a tough kid, and he seemed to be mostly ok but a little shook up. He was about to say something but was interrupted by Pat Vizzone yelling "COPS!"

12

FOURTH OF JULY: THE FINALE

I'm not saying that I had they kind of familiarity with the police at the level of Pat Vizzone or the Barlows, but I had been in situations similar to this before. The wild card here was my dad. Normally I would have just grabbed my brother and started running, but I was a little confused by the power dynamics. He was an adult, and my dad, but I wasn't sure if that was a benefit to us right now or not. I couldn't figure out if I should wait for him to tell us what to do, or just do what I was going to do and hope he came along. I had zero reference for any of this, and I had to make a decision in the next five seconds. I was leaning towards wait for my dad to do something when he said," Crap!" and then looked at me and asked, "Which way are we running?"

Pat Vizzone was grabbing all the fireworks he could. I grabbed my brother, turned to my dad and said, "This way," and headed off for the far corner of the field. I knew there was a spot in the fence big enough for us all to get under. Also, the cops were facing the wrong way on the side street, it would take them forever to get around to the other side of the field and by then we would be out in the alley behind our houses. They had started sweeping the field with the side-mounted spotlight, so no time like the present to get the hell out of there.

We booked it. Me, my brother, and Ricky in front followed by my dad and Pat Vizzone. Behind us something big blew, we could feel the shock wave. Pat ran up alongside us and said, "Figured we could use a little distraction," without breaking stride.

It looked like it worked. Everyone had scattered for the edges of the field and the cops were focused on where that last one went off in the center. They couldn't decide who or what to chase and which direction to go I guess. I wasn't about to wait around to see how it played out. A couple other people had picked up on the idea and had thrown some orange smoke bombs, and someone else lit what sounded like a full belt of firecrackers behind in the field, which was quickly descending into smoke and chaos.

We reached the corner, and I grabbed the bottom of the chain link fence that was loose, pulled it up, and shoved my brother under it. Normally he would have rolled right through like nothing, but he was still a little dazed and needed a hand. Next through was Ricky, who grabbed my brother once he was under and kept heading for the alley across the street. My dad came through next, and he stopped and grabbed the armload of fireworks Pat handed him and then Pat went under, followed by me last.

A quick-step hunched over jog into the alley across

the street and then we were in the Vizzones' backyard. My dad gave Pat back the fireworks.

"Thanks"

"Thanks for calling out the cops, I never even saw them."

"Me either. But I could smell 'em."

It felt good to laugh off some of the adrenaline. It was pretty dark back there, but we were able to give my brother a quick once over and while he seemed to be OK, his shirt was toast. The Crazy Cracker had melted a hole in the front of the mesh jersey, but it was too dark to see the full extent of the damage. How he didn't get burned was beyond me.

"Go in and change that shirt right now. Put that one in the laundry room I'll get it later," my dad said to my brother, who seemed to be back with us firing on all cylinders. He looked back at me questioning.

"We'll be here don't worry. I'll wait for you." I told him. Reassured, he went around the corner of the yard, down the side along the Hoffmans' garage to cut through and hop the fence.

The noise from the field had died down. Everyone had scattered, and since we knew the cops were around it wasn't a good idea to get back to lighting stuff off just yet, which was why we were all a little surprised to hear what sounded like a muffled ground display going off. Someone just did not give a damn. Mr. Kaminski maybe? I quickly ruled him out, because while I doubted he was as worried about the police as we were, this sounded like it was in a backyard or down the alley a ways, and he was out front.

Pat and Ricky edged out towards the alley, looking first back down towards the field, then they turned and looked back down towards the other end of the block, and something surprised them both. I looked at my dad and we went over to see what was up.

Three doors down, it looked like there was a fireworks show happening *inside* the Barlows' garage, and there was a lot of smoke starting to come out of what looked like a broken window on the side facing us.

Ricky and I looked at each other but didn't say anything. I don't know what he was thinking, but I was thinking about felony arson and how old I would be when I got out of jail. But then I had another thought - what the hell was going off in there? If it was us, all we sent in was two rockets and a stink bomb taped together. Whatever was happening in there seemed like it was still gaining momentum. We could also see that there was clearly a fire that had started in there and it was gaining momentum as well.

"I don't know what that is, and it wasn't us, but I don't want to get caught up in it so I'm out of here," Pat said, and headed back around the front of the house.

My dad watched him go and then turned to me and Ricky, "He's right, let's get out of here. Back out front!" We headed around the side of the Vizzones' garage into Ricky's back yard, where we met my brother who was back out after a quick shirt change. We just grabbed him, wordlessly redirected him and walked out front, where we all casually sat down on our front porch and were immediately hit with a bottle rocket.

The Smedleys had not run out of rockets or beer yet, which was impressive. It was getting late. My heart was pounding, and all I wanted was to go inside to my room and hope it all blew over, but I knew that would be really suspicious so didn't. I looked over at Ricky, and he was not looking too good either. From far away we heard sirens. My dad went in to grab a beer, and we had a chance to talk:

"What happened? Was that us?" Ricky was wide eyed and more nervous than I had ever seen him.

"Maybe? I don't know man and it's too late to do anything about it now. We need to make sure that candle and stuff is gone from under the deck, but we can't go back there now."

"Yeah, we gotta play dumb out here like everyone else. I think I can get it later when I let the dog out before bed."

From up on the roof the Smedleys had noticed the fire "Holy sh..hey guys, someone's garage must have gotten hit, it's going up! Over there!" They were pointing to an orange glow that was coming from the back of the houses.

My dad came out with a beer and said, "Let's go check it out, from a safe distance," and we headed back out into the alley. I was having a tough time acting casual.

The whole neighborhood that was still up and out, which was most of it, had migrated from the front yards to the back yards to watch the fire, and the people who had ditched the cops in the field were all out there too. It was getting pretty good, I have to admit. The roof was intact, but there were flames licking around it in several spots from under the eaves, and there were still explosions and what seemed like roman candles going off. Every once in a while a glowing blue or green ball would shoot out from the fire. There was nothing else around that could catch from the blaze so I don't think anyone was worried about safety or protecting property.

Except for Mr. Barlow, who had arrived out back recently and was watching his garage burn with both of his hands on the top of his head like he was waiting to be arrested.

The firetrucks rolled up and started pulling hoses and gearing up. "You been lighting fireworks?" one of the firefighters asked Mr. Barlow.

"No. I just got here."

Just then what sounded like a whole brick of firecrackers started going off in the middle of the fire, followed by several bottle rockets blowing up through where the roof would have been.

"Were you *storing* fireworks in there?" The cop who had arrived on scene, possibly the same one who had chased us out of the park, was asking questions and watching Mr. Barlow intently now.

"The door lock is broken; I don't know what someone did in there."

"Are you suggesting someone broke in…to store their fireworks in there?" the cop asked with a hint of sarcasm in his tone.

"I'm not suggesting anything to you officer. I don't know anything about fireworks in that garage, I just got here," he replied.

The fire department was hosing down both the Barlows' garage and the surrounding garages and lawns and stuff I suppose to help prevent any spread, but they were far enough away that I don't think there was any real danger of that. I think they were just kinda waiting for the fireworks to stop going off, or at least slow down a bit before trying to directly address the garage itself beyond pouring water on it from a safe distance. I don't blame them; it was pretty loud and since no one was hurt or going to be hurt there wasn't any real rush. The garage was clearly a total loss by now anyway.

I was scared. I felt like every single move I made was suspicious. It seemed like the cops were trying to watch me out of the corner of their eyes or something. It didn't look like they were paying us any more attention than any other kid who was out there watching the fire, and there was actually a pretty good bunch, but it felt like it.

Details from all those FBI books I had read were coming back to me. All those agents, resources, months of relentless observation, investigation, evidence gathering. They were going to drop the hammer on me and Ricky, I was sure of it. They were probably watching right now. I had to get myself together. My mind was racing through every wild scenario and now was not a great time to be doing that. This was not good…

But on the other hand, we had no idea what had actually happened because we weren't there when the fire had started. For all we know something else from someone else, like the Smedleys, could have landed on that garage and set it up. Both James and Kelly (and probably several other people) had reasons for vengeance, and torching a garage seemed like something that was in both of their wheelhouses. Maybe Mr. Barlow torched his own garage for all we knew. I mean, all this seemed pretty thin seeing as how we had pointed two rockets with a stink bomb taped to them directly at it, but you never know, probabilities are strange. I suppose the mind will grasp at anything to avoid having to face an awful truth sometimes.

Also, while we didn't specifically picture this scenario, the whole reason we had done things the way we had, all that testing and remote ignition and all that, was to provide cover that now we needed and seemed like we might be ok because of all that, although I was still freaking out. As long as we got underneath Ricky's deck cleared out before any investigations happened, we should be fine.

It didn't make me feel any better about what had happened though. We didn't know everything that was in the garage. We knew James had his BMX stuff in there and that was gone for sure now, but there could have been treasured Barlow family heirlooms, or collections, or projects Mr. Barlow had been developing for years, or who knows what. I didn't want to destroy that. I didn't even really want to burn the garage down, at least not at first, I was just mad, but unfortunately here we were. I suppose we just weren't prepared for overachievement at this level.

Oddly enough, James Barlow, the one person who you would think would be around for something like a garage burning down, was nowhere to be seen. There were a lot of other people out and around now, and it was turning into a weird social event in the alley. People started passing out beers. There were little groups having conversations, including Mr. Barlow, who was also having a beer and seemed to be enjoying himself.

The atmosphere had an effect on me and Ricky because we were a little more relaxed now. They weren't actively investigating, questioning people, scanning the crowd for suspects; maybe a couple of kids who look a little too interested and kinda guilty. Nope none of that. The cops were just standing around watching the firefighters make sure it was out like the rest of us.

Eventually my dad came over and said, "OK you two, I think that's enough excitement for one night, let's pack it in." so we said our "laters" to Ricky and Andy and the other guys and headed home. My brother seemed completely unfazed by his earlier experience, which was very in-character for him. He was not the type to milk an injury, mostly due to the fact that he had such an appetite for adventure combined with a low level of self-preservation that he had a surprising amount of these types of incidents, so he just accepted it as part of the territory he had chosen to exist in.

I had a hard time falling asleep that night. It felt like the day had started a week ago. I was tired but too wired, probably still going from all the excess adrenaline I had in me. I was scared about the garage, happy about the All-Star game, and proud of holding my own in a real fireworks fight. I lay there listening to the distant pops of fireworks still going off for a long time, trying to make sense of the chain of events that started with a parade and ending running from the cops with my dad after setting my brother on fire with illegal fireworks and then watching a garage I may have had a role in igniting burn down together.

13
FIFTH OF JULY: THE AFTERMATH

The day after the Fourth of July was also a big day for us. We would go out to all the spots people had been blowing stuff off the night before and scavenge. Lots of times if you lit an entire pack of firecrackers at once (the fuses were all wrapped together in a way that you could) the blast of the others would blow one or two free, wick intact and all. Even the ones without wicks that were duds still had some value to us. You could cut them in half to expose the powder inside and light it directly, which would fizzle and spray sparks, or you could harvest the fuel and make it into a new larger explosive, theoretically. We never quite mastered the art of creating fireworks in this way, which in retrospect was probably a good thing, but it seemed our success rate for the homemade repurposed ones was exceptionally low. Didn't really matter though. These spares were free and were part of what kept us stocked until next year. This was like our fall harvest for the winter months with no fireworks events. We needed supplies for our booby traps, distractions, retaliation, experiments and whatever else and it just wasn't possible to connect in February and get a brick of firecrackers. No one had any.

I got dressed and then ate a quick bowl of cereal in the kitchen. It was Tuesday, so my dad had already headed off to work, and my mom had left a note saying she would be back later. That was good. I had been thinking and plotting and planning until late in the night, and now I was focused on where I needed to go and what I needed to do. I did not need the added challenge of trying to dodge my mom.

My brother was already outside, on the front porch talking to Andy. I gave a quick head nod as I passed down the steps on my way next door to get Ricky.

"You going searching today?"

"Yeah, in a little bit."

"Can we come with you?"

"Yeah sure. Andy, make sure your mom knows you're out with us, I don't want to hear about it from her again." I still wasn't exactly sure how it had been my fault, but I didn't really want to discuss it further with her either.

"OK – what should I tell her?"

What are you asking me for, I said to myself. "Just say we're going to be at Emerson, which is not a lie because we are going to be at Emerson, and nothing else." It was good enough. I doubt it mattered. I think Mrs. Kaminski had enough to deal with being in charge of five kids *and* Mr. Kaminski, and sometimes didn't have the time and energy to get into the details. Andy just needed to be reasonably convincing and not make her life more complicated and keep me out of it.

I came around the back of the Hoffmans' house and you could smell the wet burned smell of the Barlows' garage. I could see over into their yard from the deck. Now in the daylight it didn't look as festive as it had last night. The far corner was still standing, just two partial walls, and where the rest used to be was just a pile of burnt wet stuff. I could see what looked like some boxes, and there was a tool bench. The roof had come down on it so that was covering almost everything else. It was surrounded by that yellow "police/caution" tape, which gave it a crime scene look, and that added to my already uneasy feeling. I tapped on the deck door, and Ricky popped around the corner into his living room.

"Hey. Been waiting for you," he said as he let me in.

"Anyone else home?"

"No, at work."

He reached down under the coffee table and held up the nub of taper candle, which he put on the table. He then reached down and pulled out the rocket with the bottle rocket, fishing weight, and stink bomb, still taped together, still with fuses, and put them on the table too. "I got it last night after everyone left. The candle must have gone out. The rest of the stuff out there I just put back how it was, wiped the dirt with a branch to cover any marks."

It had never gone off. It wasn't us. For once a technical issue and catastrophic failure had actually saved our asses. I was relieved, but at the same time I was strangely a little upset. While I was glad we didn't have to worry about getting jammed up for something serious, I had also been kinda proud that we had gotten back at James in spectacular fashion, and now that it turned out we didn't have anything to do with it, it was a little deflating.

I still didn't *feel* like we were out of the woods entirely, but at least there was no evidence that could be tied back to us laying around. "So it really wasn't us? Did you see anything? How did the fire start then?"

"I don't know. Everything was still set up exactly as we left it, so I don't think anyone saw. I'm having a hard time believing the fire was just a random firework though, there must have been something in the garage that was really flammable. Like, how many times have we tried to start fires using rockets on purpose with no luck? Or remember that time Rob Kelton shot one into the leaf pile in the street? That didn't go right up either."

"There was other stuff going off in that garage too," I nodded, "that's what's confusing. I wonder if James set off a ground display in there or something. Do you think they are going to investigate?"

"Maybe. My dad said that's what insurance is for, so I guess someone from the insurance company will have to check it out. I don't know about the cops. Doesn't matter though, there's no way to trace anything back to us. Besides, it turns out we didn't even do anything, and I don't know if they could get us just because we wanted to but totally failed. Relax."

"I can't relax, I feel like everyone knows and they're just waiting to get us coming out of the movie theater or we're going to get grabbed into a van in the 7-11 parking lot or something." Ricky turned his head to look at me. "I know, I know; I can't help it. Let's get out of here, the earlier we get to the field the better anyway."

I still felt nervous, but Ricky was right. We hadn't actually done anything. Maybe it wasn't even that big of a deal, or not a big enough deal for the police and insurance people to care that much. There hadn't even been any cars in there. If anything, they would be looking at Mr. Barlow. Now that we had a clearer picture of the situation, it did seem to have all the ingredients for some type of scam or insurance fraud, and he did sorta seem the type.

We headed back outside. I hollered at my brother and Andy to come with us if they were coming with us and cut back through the alley. It always looks so different the morning after. The light is harsher, the damage more apparent, the litter visible. Anywhere someone had lit something that blew big on the concrete had left a scorch mark, and there were plenty of scorch marks up to where the water from the fire department had washed them away. This was just in the alley; we weren't even in the field yet.

No one else was in the field when we got there. There were two main areas to search, the first being the packed dirt area along the school wall where we played Hotbox, and the second was out in the field. The best firecracker spot was along the wall, so we hit there first and did pretty well. There was a ton of paper. I don't know if people came back after the cops chased us off or there was just a lot that got set off before and during the excitement, but it looked like easily a few bricks in total had been lit.

Out in the field was a different story. A more forensic approach was needed, because anything out there was probably bigger, and could potentially still go off depending upon what it was and what it had been subjected to, so we wanted to be a little more careful. It was all for nothing though, outside of a few unexploded rockets there wasn't anything useful left out there.

Instead of cutting back through the alley into Rickys back yard we went around the long way, to check out the front of the block, retracing Mrs. Vizzone's steps from last night. This was ground zero for where the Smedleys had been firing, and it looked it. In the daylight it was pretty amazing how many red sticks were laying all over out there. Those guys had sent down a truly impressive number of rockets.

There were some other kids out now, and moms picking up lawn chairs and card tables and empties left out from the night before. There was nothing to scavenge, we were more or less just surveying the damage and bumping around. Everyone was talking about the garage fire.

The general consensus in the neighborhood was that it was either one of the Barlows themselves or the Smedleys, or a combination of both, that had caused the fire. I made no comments because I was still afraid of incriminating myself somehow, although I don't know what I would be guilty of at this point. My nerves were not handling any of this well.

Ant came out and joined our little group by the streetlight in front of his house.

"Hey dill hole. Where were you last night?"

"Firebombing my a-hole neighbor's garage." He tossed a rock up at the light. "Where were you guys? Lighting sparklers with your mom?"

"Haha nope, with *your* mom."

"Shut up. I had to take my little sister to the show at the high school and it took forever to get back here, it was already burning when we got back. Did you see what happened?"

Ricky and I both said "no" immediately. There was a long pause and I said, "We were over in the field."

Ant looked at me, and for a second it looked like he was going to say something else, but then thought better of it and said, "My dad, he was talking to Mr. Barlow last night, in the backyard, I was there, and he said that it was actually not such a bad thing. He said that all he had in there was a bunch of products he couldn't sell, and this was better than a tax write off, whatever that is. Supposedly insurance is going to pay for a new garage, and he can claim all the stuff that was in there. After whatever a deductible is."

"Really? Huh. Well, I guess that's how it works. So, uh … does he know how it went up?" This was the real question, and I was trying not to act nervous or guilty, although now I had no reason to be. It's not easy to shake those feelings, especially when you have spent the past ten hours considering the reality that you may have to escape from the police and live life on the run as a fugitive garage arsonist.

"Not sure what started it, but he said he had like half a pallet stacked up with fireworks he snagged cheap off some guy he knew who got busted by the cops and couldn't move it out of his storage space. He dumped it all in the garage and I guess was going to just hold it until next Fourth of July and sell it then, but something must have somehow set it all off. It was weird. He wasn't even mad at all, actually seemed like he was kinda happy. Like he said, he gets a nice new garage and a check for everything that was in it, so he's probably gonna end up on the positive side of a deal here." I have to say, we didn't see that coming.

He must have wanted to keep the fireworks hidden

from his wife and kids so went with the "security in plain sight" method of just stacking them in with all the other boxes in there, and he was right, really. Why would anyone pay any attention to more unmarked cardboard boxes amongst the piles and pallets of boxes in there already. It was a two-car garage and there was no room for even one car in there. Last time I had been in there it was just a couple narrow little pathways between pallets of boxes of Pet Sticks and God knows what else he had "picked up at a discount" that was stored in there. That garage was ready to go up at the suggestion of flame.

I'm not sure if knowing any of this in advance would have changed things or not. I am pretty sure we still would have tried something, and it probably would have involved the garage and fireworks, although sitting there thinking about it I could see maybe considering a different approach if we knew that the garage was essentially full of accelerants, fuel, and explosives. Or maybe not. James had thrown two m-1000 quarter sticks at me, I can't say I had been deeply concerned about his property or safety.

None of this had gone as expected, and we should have taken it as a lesson about life and moved on, but we felt kinda cheated. James Barlow threw a brick through my garage window, and a bomb at me, and we retaliated in what we thought had ended up being unplanned yet spectacular fashion and then it turned out it wasn't us and now we were strangely disappointed. It was so unfair. It did explain where James had been getting all those quality fireworks though. He must have found his dad's stash and started helping himself.

After dinner that night, I was in my room laying on

my bed reading when I heard my mom calling from the basement:

"Boys. Come here please."

Not good. It was that calm yet angry tone. I was trying to think what she could have discovered in the laundry room that would be trouble, but I came up blank. Maybe I left a lighter or something in my shorts? Or my brother did? Possible, but doubtful. I couldn't see either of us being that careless. Maybe it was something stupid like leaving the water running in there or …. I don't know. And that was the worst type of situation to go into – you had no idea what you were about to get busted for so no real chance to come up with some kind of plausible excuse or reason in advance.

I was not expecting to see my mom holding up my brother's "no. 7" mesh jersey. Only it wasn't really a "no.7" anymore because most of the front was a melted hole. I was still not processing the full gravity of the situation and for a second I thought the dryer had melted it. Then my brother came in and the look on his face suddenly triggered a memory of him tumbling in the field with the Crazy Cracker exploding on him and I knew we were in deep trouble.

"Can you explain this please?"

We had no clue how much she already knew. Adding to the complexity was the fact that my dad had been there when it got burned and we weren't sure if she knew that. Worse than getting busted by mom would be ratting out Dad and getting him busted too, so we had to be careful here.

"Dad told me to take it off "

There goes that. My brother had effectively sealed

our escape route, now we had to try and minimize the damage by …well, minimizing the damage. Gloss over the facts, let some minimal details out, hope we can control the narrative and spin it in a way that doesn't get us banned from the Fourth of July and fireworks for the rest of our lives….

That was when my dad walked into the laundry room. He looked at the shirt but didn't say anything, his expression remained unchanged. I started to improvise:

"Oh, uh yeah that. So yesterday we were watching some guys light some stuff off with everyone else and I think some sparks flew a bit … you know and … ah some landed on him and so we just wanted to be sure it was ok so Dad told him to change his shirt and checked him out and uh…so …."

I had lost. I knew it. I wasn't buying it, she wasn't buying it, and I had painted myself in a corner with the story because there was no way out after saying Dad checked him out. Now he was on the hook. My mom turned to my dad and said, "You checked him out?"

This was it. The ball was squarely in his court. He could just throw us to the wolves and walk away from it. He had a lot of options really; he could deny it, say he couldn't see in the dark, say he told us not to, but we did anyway. He didn't have to go down with this ship at all.

"Oh yeah, that. It was no big deal, one of the kids got a little too close to him with a sparkler and sprayed his shirt a bit. That jersey material can get melty, so I told him to go change his shirt. It must have just smoldered in here for a bit because I didn't see a hole like that when he went in."

Dad was not giving us up, but it was probably

because if my mom made us retrace the events all the way back to who lit the Crazy Cracker it would not be good for him either. What he said was technically true, in the darkness none of us had seen the actual size and extent of the burn hole on my brother. Now standing there with my mom we realized just how lucky he had been, but he was always narrowly avoiding serious permanent injuries like that so at the same time we felt like it was par for the course. We couldn't express any of that anyway. Time to shut up and let dad handle it.

"You left a burning shirt in a pile of laundry? Unattended?" Well ok maybe not totally out of it. As mentioned previously, my mom had a real phobia of unattended fire. My dad was walking the thinnest of lines right now.

"I told him to toss it in the laundry sink. Where did you find it? In the laundry basket?" Turning to my brother, "You put it in the sink like I told you right?"

I saw an opening and shoved through it. "This morning I came down to check on my All-Star uniform … see it's still soaking right there … and I saw it in the sink, but I thought he had just tossed it in here and it landed there by accident, so I dropped it in the basket with everything else."

Ball back in mom's court now. It was up to her. She could continue pursuing the truth or just be grateful we were all unharmed and leave it at that. Uncertainty and tension hung in the room. Nothing happened while she was processing. We all just stood there nervously waiting our fate. Finally, she spoke:

"Well, you should have told me," to my dad.

"I'm glad no one was hurt," to my brother.

"Take this outside and put it in the garbage can, I

don't want it in the house, it stinks," to me, while handing me the melted remains of the jersey.

That was…it? My mom had turned her back on us and gone back to loading up the washing machine. We looked over at my dad who was motioning towards the door with his thumb. Me and my brother scooted out.

Safe at home, again.

14
KICK THE CAN

We were sitting in the Mustang in Ricky's garage. Summer vacation had long ago hit the point where you couldn't differentiate the days of the week easily, but we knew it wasn't the weekend because there were no dads in garages, no lawnmowers running. Summer or not, they were at work during the week leaving the moms in charge and the kids free in the neighborhood.

It was not uncommon for my mom to see us at breakfast, not see us again until 5:30pm for dinner, and then we would be back in around 9:30-10:30pm, whenever my folks decided it was time for us to come in, which was either before or after they watched the news. If they had friends over for dinner, we would get to stay out a little later, and if it was neighborhood friends over for dinner we could stay out real late because everyone would be hanging out in someone's back yard so we could just be free as long as we remained out of sight/out of mind.

"So, who's going to be there? My parents, yours, I think Keltons and Swensons?"

"Yup. Not sure about everyone else, but it's going to be a big party though. Not block party big but most of the people from our end of the block will be there."

In our minds the block was divided into four sections: our side of the block, the other side of the block, our end of the block and the other end of the block. Interestingly enough, though there were no formal dividing lines or landscape features that would designate boundaries, it seemed that the adults had kinda fallen into recognizing this grouping, although I would guess it was more due to proximity than anything else.

Tonight's event was going to be at the Gundersons, who were not at our end of the block, but they used to be. They had lived in the two-flat next to us, and when a single-family home went up for sale at the other end they bought it and moved down there (clearing the path for the Smedley boys to move in next to us, for which I am forever grateful). They were the hemp cloth/homemade granola types, recycling before it was city mandated, bike riding whenever possible. I liked them, Mrs. G was from Japan, was an amazing cook, and had endless funny stories, so it was going to be a good time when they invited you over for dinner.

However, tonight we were not going to be eating whatever exotic cuisine Mrs. G was creating, because we were not invited. This was a "grown-ups only" event. They had these every so often, I think primarily so they could take a break from having to deal with us and enjoy a nice dinner without having to break up any fights or answer questions about why we couldn't have a pet monkey or why we couldn't make our own gunpowder in the garage, even though we could easily get the ingredients and totally could.

"Man, we should do something tonight, everyone will be around."

"We need to find out who. We could play touch football if we got enough for two sides and an all-time quarterback."

"We could, but remember what happened with Carla last time?"

Carla was Ant's little sister, although "little" was more of an age designation than a size descriptor. She was quite athletic but a little bit stockier than the other girls in the neighborhood, and not unaware of the difference in her size and strength abilities relative to the rest of us. She was extremely competitive, did not like losing, and did not have a good concept of "laying up" on someone especially when playing touch football on asphalt. This is a long way of saying she beat our asses, badly, and I was not super interested in reliving the experience, especially in the dark.

"Oh. Yeah. No. No, not a good idea. Besides, it will get dark too fast, can't play. "

"Kick the Can? We haven't played that since the block party last year."

"Yeah. Yeah, I'm up for that if there's enough people. Let's go see if we can find out who's going to be around." A quick walk through the neighborhood and we had a pretty solid number - 11 confirmed, possibly four more if the Dimopoulos's got home from their church thing early enough — who were going to meet us under the tree in front of Ricky's house tonight.

Kick the Can, for those who have never played, is hide and seek on a larger scale, with a few twists. We usually played with two or three seekers instead of one, because we liked to use large boundaries which would be way too much ground for one person to cover. This kept the game moving and added a bit more of the chase element, which was a lot more exciting than the waiting in a hiding place by yourself for a long time element.

If you were caught, you had to go to "jail," which was our front porch. The only way out of jail was to have one of the other hiders (we called them "runners") physically kick the can, which was usually somewhere on the lawn or sidewalk in front of Ricky's house, next door to jail at my house. If you managed to kick the can without getting tagged, everyone in jail was free.

The game was over when there was only one runner left free. They won, and the person who had been in jail the longest was the next seeker and got to pick the rest of their team, although we tried to mix it up so that no one got stuck chasing after everyone all the time. You would never be seeking more than three times a session unless you wanted to, just keeping it fun for everyone, although it wasn't that big of a deal. We mostly did it so that the younger kids got a fair chance, and it worked out.

It was a fun game anytime you had enough people, but we liked it best at night. We knew almost all of the hiding spots and really most yards and garages throughout the neighborhood, so making it dark took that advantage away a bit when searching for people. It also added an extra bit of danger, which of course we welcomed. Not being able to see was a challenge for the runners too, especially if you were the type who liked garage roofs or trees for hiding spots. Flashlights weren't really used much because it could give away your position, so if you crawled into a spot next to a garage and turned to find yourself facing a semi-awake opossum who was not thrilled to see you, as happened to my brother, you had a whole other set of issues to deal with outside of not getting tagged, such as not getting rabies.

The boundaries, or really the lack of boundaries, were what made it the most fun though. Usually in-bounds was our side of the block, all the way down to the other end. You could go in the alley, but not to the other side. Inside houses was off limits, but other than that nothing else was. Trees, roofs, porches, garages, whatever; if you could get yourself in, up on, or behind it, it was fair game. You couldn't lock a door, but if you got in through other means and the door was locked that was OK, although uncommon. We didn't have a ton of respect for private property, but we also didn't want to get jammed up breaking into someone's garage for a game of Kick the Can. It also depended on who's garage. Never went in the Barlows', never worried about going into the Pavliks', but for the most part we just didn't. To me, hiding inside felt like a cheat and I wanted to beat you by hanging in a tree over your head or something, silently and motionless, like a ninja.

We loved ninjas, they were the natural extension of our obsession with spies and secret operations, and Kick the Can was our favorite opportunity to test out some of those methods and tactics we had learned from our extensive ninja book collection. You couldn't get these at the library. You had to go to the local semi-sketchy martial arts "dojo" that sold nunchucks and throwing stars and all the cool yet completely impractical ninja weapons.

I was obsessed with throwing stars and grappling hooks, and of course was expressly forbidden from owning either by my mom. This didn't stop me from owning throwing stars, I just had to keep them hidden, but I don't think my parents had much to worry about as far as me doing any real damage with them. They were plenty sharp, but also plenty difficult to control and easy to lose, so all we ended up doing was standing in the alley and throwing them at a section of wooden fence we had garbage picked and leaned up against Ricky's garage.

Grappling hooks were another matter. They did not sell them at the local dojo, and I didn't think I would be able to order one from a catalog and keep it hidden from my folks. Having a package arrive for me and then not telling anyone what was in it would set off my mom's alarm bells for sure. Plus, they weren't cheap, and in all the scenarios I concocted in my head there was always a good chance of not being able to retrieve it and I didn't have the budget for that sort of thing. Many times I had imagined creeping along a roofline like the garages across the alley, all in black, rope and grappling hook slung across my body, pockets full of tools and weapons and spy gear, ready to ... well that part I never really did work out. I figured once I was geared up the work would come to me.

As much as we were interested in all the gear and weapons, we weren't as interested in the martial arts part of the martial arts. Joining a dojo and taking lessons took money we didn't have. Also, it seemed a little lackluster when it came to results. All my friends who were taking karate or whatever didn't seem to be much better off for it regardless of their belt color.

I had taken a "lesson" once from Rob Kelton who was a purple belt in something or other (it wasn't karate). He told me he could show me some basics, and to meet in his back yard. When I showed up, he was all geared up in this white kung fu suit, and said he was going to show me defensive moves first, as these were the most useful. I disagreed, but whatever, you get what you pay for I guess.

"I'm going to demonstrate first," he said, "I want you to attack when I say go," and then he got into what I now understand to be a horse stance. This is a very fundamental stance found in many martial arts forms and it looks like what it sounds like: you kinda crouch a bit and make two fists in front or your waistline area, like you're holding the reins of a horse. What it looked like to me was an invitation to kick him in the nuts, and when he said "Go!" I accepted that invitation and kicked him in the nuts, which put an end to both that lesson and the prospect of any future lessons.

The most coveted and seemingly unattainable of all ninja gear was what I would consider "evasive distraction options." These were like big firecrackers and smoke bombs that went off on impact, no fuses or lighting needed. Allegedly the smoke bombs were filled with some kind of irritant as well. There were also envelopes of powder that could be thrown in enemies' eyes, but since it didn't involve explosions we weren't as interested in that one and it wasn't hard to achieve at all.

Those giant snap-and-pops though. There were like our white whale. No one sold them. We had never even seen them for sale in any catalog or mentioned anywhere. What would you even call them, ninja pocket bombs? None of our books had any in-depth information (probably due to legal reasons). Early on we realized this was going to be something we had to make ourselves. Ninety percent of all the dud firecrackers we picked up on the fifth of July were used in our attempts to create them. Never worked, which was probably for the best (*Author's note — I found out later in life that they do still exist and are used in the railroad industry as a signal for trains backing up, they put them on the tracks and when the wheel rolls over it, bang! Imagine a snap-and-pop that could blow your arm off. That is why they are not sold anywhere*).

My brother and I were home by about five o'clock, which was early but when there was a dinner partly like this we had to hear the "you're on your own/be responsible/check in with us we're just down the block if you need us" speech before my folks left, and then we could make some hot dogs, watch TV while we ate dinner which was a big treat and then get back out there. But first we needed to gear up.

Even though we didn't have the best ninja gear and spy gadgets, we still had some pretty good stuff. Because we didn't always have opportunities to use it, when something like this was happening, if there was the slightest possibility that you could try a piece of gear out, you brought it. Plus, after being in situations previously and wishing you had one thing or another you tend to start building up an inventory of useful items. Most of us had a kit of some kind, typically just enough to fit in a small backpack, cargo pants or a utility belt. My brother had an army canteen belt he used that had all these different pouches and things clipped to it, and he wasn't the only one who preferred the belt approach.

Batman wasn't our favorite superhero, but we agreed with him on a lot of things.

I preferred the fatigues/cargo pants approach. In my used jungle camos purchased from the Army Navy surplus store I had a lighter, my Swiss army camper knife which was awesome because it had a saw, a notebook and small pencil, a roll of black electrical tape, two pieces of white chalk in a plastic baggie, one pack of firecrackers, twenty yards of twelve-pound test fishing line neatly wrapped, ten yards of clothesline-sized cotton rope which had started out white but was now dirty gray/brown and had a 4 ounce fishing weight tied to one end, a pack of matches, a small penlight like doctors use, a blue bandana, my wallet, and my lucky rock. I looped my watch through a front beltloop and tucked it into the top of my front pocket. A final pat down and I was good to go.

We got back out as the sun was just starting to turn the clouds pink and orange. By 6:45 everyone was out and it was a good group. Almost all the neighborhood kids were there except those who were too young; they were all watching movies at the Walters who lived upstairs from us. Their girls were old enough and responsible enough to babysit, and smart enough to not be running around doing stupid things with us all the time, so the little kids all got dropped there.

"Ok, so jail is Peaches' front porch, can is in my front yard. Everyone good with that?" Ricky was laying out the rules.

"How many seekers?"

"Uh – how many people we got? One, two, three, four….twelve, thirteen, fourteen, and me is fifteen? Damn, who's *not* here? OK I think three seekers, right?"

"Yeah, that sounds good."

"Boundaries are this whole side, all the way down to the end, alley is in, across the alley is out."

"Apartments at the other end?" There was a large apartment complex that ran perpendicular to the end of our block, dead ending the alley. It had hallways and porches and different levels, almost like a little mini neighborhood in there, and you could get around pretty much unseen from the outside if you knew the layout, but it was not without risks.

"Out. The building manager is a total a-hole, he chased us with a bat and said he was going to call the cops last time."

"OK. So should we go other side of the street too or think we got enough space?"

The other side of the street was interesting. It was still your typical suburban block, but there was no alley on that side. The back yards butted up to a strange corridor between back yard fences that I suppose was some kind of utility easement or something. It was like a six foot wide gap full of leaves and yard waste and whatever else people had dumped back there over the years. Nothing awesome, just a few spare tires, an old couch that had deteriorated to just frame and springs, miscellaneous rock piles.

"Eh … let's keep it over here to start and see how it goes. That work? Across the street is out of bounds."

Everyone agreed to that. To get things going and prevent a lengthy series of rock-paper-scissors and eenie-meenie-minee-mo's, me and Ricky volunteered to be seekers, and Ant's sister Carla lost the rock-paper-scissors tournament so she was our third.

"OK, we're counting to thirty then coming after you.

Getting caught out of bounds means you are out for the rest of the game. No time limit? No time limit, it goes to last man standing. Everyone ready?" Me, Ricky and Carla put our heads against the tree in front of Ricky's house and started counting out loud "One…two…three…" and everyone else took off. Game on.

We got to thirty, and since there was no one that needed babysitting in jail yet we all took off looking. The three of us were experienced Kick the Can players so there wasn't much need to discuss tactics. Ricky and I probably knew most of the regular hiding spots on the block, and Carla was pretty good too, so this was going to get down to the chase part pretty quickly, which is what happened. I liked having Carla on our team though, she was a great protector of both the captives in jail and the can. She had surprising closing speed so Ricky and I ended up kinda funneling the rest of the runners back towards jail and then letting her pick them off when they tried to kick the can.

The first two games were pretty routine. They were also a little quick, more like big games of tag, which was fun but also took the hiding/stealth element almost entirely out of the game. We decided to include the other side of the block in the boundaries as well to spread things out a bit and make it more interesting. The sun had almost completely set by now and the streetlights were on out front, but there weren't any alley lights, so the backyards and alleys were dark.

This time the seekers were my brother, Ant, and Timbo, another experienced group. They put their heads against the tree and started counting and we all took off running to hide. Having the other side of the block in bounds gave us a lot more hiding options, but there were also some drawbacks. The biggest issue was the street itself; it became a giant no-man's land. If you were moving and wanted to cross the street there was no cover whatsoever. There weren't even any cars parked out there or anything so you would be completely exposed.

The other twist with hiding on the other side of the street was the no alley situation. This made it a little more challenging to move across yards and behind the houses because there weren't any gates or easy alley access like our side had. It was hopping fences or crawling through bushes or both. The Swensons had a high wooden fence that their dogs had managed to dig under so they put a chain-link along the inside perimeter of it, creating a double fence that really sucked trying to negotiate, plus their dogs were totally mental. They would start barking at literally anything, like the wind or shadows, and while they were mostly friendly with us we had never tested out what they would do if you suddenly dropped into their yard and weren't interested in finding out what would happen either.

Personally, I liked that side of the street, even with the challenges presented. I think that's why I liked it, specifically because it wasn't easy to navigate. I knew that you could get from one end to the other without touching the ground though. You had to hop along fences, into trees and across garage roofs, but if you knew the path it wasn't too bad. Ricky and I had trailblazed back there and were the originators of the path as far as we knew so this was pretty familiar territory.

I'm not saying that just knowing the path made it all

easy travels. There were some transition points that were a little precarious. One section you had to balance along the two-by-four that was at the top of the wooden fence for about twelve feet until there was a tree you could use for support. That was probably the riskiest part of the whole path. The trick was to focus on where you were going, not look down and not try to go too fast. Even if you did lose your balance, it was only about eight feet to the ground, so very survivable drop, unless you somehow got into the dreaded "nut spear" situation by trying to straddle the top of the fence with your off foot for balance and missing, in which case your crotch was in for a bad time.

I wasn't headed back there though. My spot was closer to the Kelton's backyard. There were a couple big trees back there and behind the apartment building over there was like a five-car garage with a long, low roof, then a driveway gap and then the Kelton's two car garage. My plan was to go fence, tree, garage, and then kinda roam around up there so I could see what was going on while keeping hidden.

Garage roofs are great hiding spots, unless you got spotted up there, in which case you were usually screwed. No easy escape route, and if you wanted to try and juke the seeker all they had to do was stay down and call for back up, and once there were two kids it was over. One could flush you while the other tagged you.

So there was that risk of easy capture if you were spotted up there, but really it was outweighed by the low likelihood of actually getting spotted up there unless you were a total dumbass. Stay low, only move if you have to move, and keep quiet, which is what I was doing up there, and it was working out well. I saw a few kids getting picked off out front. There was a clear line of sight down the driveways because they were next to each other so there was like an extra wide gap in the houses there.

There were probably five to six kids in jail, so it was time to spring them. I preferred to try and sneak up as close as I could before making a run for the can, moving from porch to bushes to tree or whatever I could use for cover.

I slid down the back of the roof to the tree, then worked around the back of the trunk until my feet felt the top of the fence, then climbed down the fence next to the garage and got low to survey the scene. It was quiet around me. I could hear the sounds of a chase from closer to the other end of the block on the other side, but I wasn't sure how many seekers were guarding the jail, and who it was, so I was going to need to get a little closer to plan my attack.

I worked my way along the edge of the apartment building and then into the bushes in front of it, which gave me clear view of the people in jail on my front porch. There were a bunch of kids up there, the seekers were an experienced bunch, they were doing a good job rounding them up, but that was about to change.

I wasn't the only one who had decided it was time or some heroics. I looked through the bushes to my right and crouched low along the side of the Frank's house, behind the rain garden they had, was Ricky. He hadn't seen me yet, but if I could get his attention, we could make quick work of setting everyone free. I was halfway tempted to just lay back and let him make a run for it and then clean up the mess if need be, but I had come all the way down here out of a great spot, I wasn't about to stop now and just watch.

Instead, I went back the way I came down the driveway, around the back of the apartments and came up along the side of the Franks' house. I couldn't move silently over fallen leaves or anything that good, but I could keep it quite enough that I surprised Ricky when I got up about ten feet behind and to his left, just into his peripheral vison, and waved. He motioned for me to close the gap and get up there with him.

"Hey dill hole. What are you thinking?"

"Thinking it's about time to bust those kids loose. How about you?"

"Your mom?"

"Dude…"

"You asked…."

"OK, really. How do you want to do this."

"Well … Ant is guarding jail and the can, but he looks like he's ranging all the way down your driveway sometimes too. I was going to wait until he got down the driveway to cross the street and then try and get in the bushes and around from the Smedley's side."

"That works I guess, as long as everyone runs either across the street or down towards the other end of the block."

"I mean, that's true but also we can't do anything about what happens once we kick the can. Although we can do something about what *we* do, which is what … head back over here? Do we even know where the other two are?"

"Not really. I think I saw Timbo heading down by Pavliks', but that was a little while ago. It doesn't really matter, there's like six kids up there, everyone's going to scatter, and he can't go in all directions. Just have to hope his backup is too far away and he doesn't lock on to us. Anyway, I feel like the longer we sit here the worse our odds get. Let's just do it and see what happens."

"Right. I'll go down my driveway into the back yard and see if I can see him, maybe distract him. Pretty sure I can beat him if he tries to hop the fence, and if he tries to go around I can hop the fence. Either way you have to kick the crap out of that can so I hear it, ok?"

Some people play with the rule that you have to yell "Jailbreak!" or "Kick the Can!" when you kick it. We did not because that is dumb. Instead, we put a few rocks into the can so it would rattle and how loud it rattled depended on how hard you kicked it.

"Ok. Let's go." We broke cover and jogged across the street, staying in a low crouch. The kids in jail saw us, but fortunately they didn't give us up. We put our fingers up over our lips to keep them quiet, and I held up my hand "wait" so they knew not to get excited and take off or make noise before we were ready.

Ricky slid into the gap in the Smedleys' bushes, and I started working my way down the driveway. The driveway was lined on both sides by the brick house walls, and it was tight, like an urban canyon. Because there wasn't much space to maneuver, I tried to keep to the side and keep low. If I was spotted here there was no option other than run, but it would mess up Ricky if I had to run back past where he was hiding, so I had to make it to the back yard undetected.

I got to the end of the driveway and peaked around the wall. Ant was in Ricky's yard next door, crouched around the corner of the house so he could see the jail, but I doubt they could see him. It was a good spot, we were lucky we had crossed the street further down where my house blocked his field of view, or he would have known we were coming.

I looked back down the driveway and could see the silhouette of Ricky's head peaking around the corner. I pointed two fingers at my eyes – "I see," then held up my index finger – "one," then made a pointing motion twice – "over there." I got a thumbs up from Ricky and he crossed the driveway towards jail and the can in the front yard.

I wanted to keep Ant back here as long as possible and ideally not looking towards the front of the house or he would see when Ricky made a run for the can and get out front too fast. He'd probably catch a couple kids making a break for it, making our jailbreak much less effective. He wasn't an idiot so no chance he would fall for the "toss a rock into the bushes" trick. I was going to have to get him another way.

I didn't have a lot of time to come up with something, Ricky was already on the move. For a second I thought about just sprinting out across the back yard, hurdling the fence track-and-field style and continuing on into the alley hoping he would chase me that way, but if the wooden gate was latched there was no way I would get back there before he caught me. Couldn't take that chance.

A better option was to be a decoy and try and bait him into moving out of position. He didn't know I knew he was there, so I decided to sneak out into the back yard acting like I didn't see him, and duck down somewhere in the yard like I was hiding. He comes over to get me and hopefully that's when Ricky gets to the can, and everyone runs.

I eased out of the cover of the side of the house and

"crept" along the back porch. I was trying to keep my head down and not look over where he was, but I could see motion over there. Pretty sure he had spotted me. On the plus side he didn't immediately jump up and start running in my direction. I think he was going to try to sneak in as close as he could or maybe hope I would sneak closer to him first before making a move. So that's what I did – I went down the path between the yard and my mom's garden, then turned my back to him and pretended to be messing with the side door to our garage, acting like it was giving me a hard time opening.

I was listening for the fence. It was a low chain link, about three feet tall, but unless you jumped it clean it would make noise. If I had to run, I had a good step or two on him if I heard the fence rattling. There was no sound. I was starting to get nervous. He had to have seen me, maybe he was waiting to see if I went into the garage, thinking I would be trapped? I could see the side of the house, and he wasn't there anymore, which was good. I had no idea where he had gone though, which was bad.

Didn't have any more time to wonder about it, because I heard the rattling of rocks in the can out front. Ricky got to it. I turned around and saw Ant standing up from where he had snuck up to the side of the fence and take off towards the front. I didn't get him into our yard so there was a chance he could still make it out front in time to catch a couple of the slower kids, but not my problem now.

I had to get out of the backyard, and there were two options – go back down the driveway and hope I could get back across the street in the chaos or stay away from all that entirely and hop the fence, heading out into the alley. I decided to head away from the action out front, so I hopped the fence, cut through the yard and went out through the gate into the alley, running right into my brother, who immediately tagged me.

"Aw man!"

"Hi." My brother was grinning and pointed towards the front of the house.

"I know, I know. Don't think you're all hot stuff, you got lucky, that's it."

"Uh huh"

"What's that supposed to mean?"

"Nothing. You believe whatever you need to if it makes you feel better."

"I ran right into you!"

"Whose fault is that?"

"You are such a wuss, I bet you were just hiding over there hoping it would be over before you had to actually catch anyone." It was on now. My brother and I had an endless trash talking dialogue going. It started when he was two years old and I was five, probably like many other siblings, and I expected it would continue for the rest of our lives.

"Look at big brother getting all mad about a game. Well … getting all mad because his little brother beat him at a game."

"You didn't beat me, I ran into you, that's different."

"Uh huh." We had reached the end of the driveway, and I went up onto our porch, put in jail by my own brother, humiliated (Not really, my brother was pretty good. He was younger than us by a few years but still managed to keep up. This was more of an older brother pride thing).

"When I get out of here I'm going to catch you and

fart on your head."

"I don't care. I've been farting in your room."

"I know. That's why I've been farting in your pillow, just keeping it even." I couldn't leave the porch, so he was safe from me for now, but he was looking at me like he wasn't sure if I was bs-ing or not. I was.

"Ok whatever. I'm going to go, have fun in jail loser."

"I'll be out soon enough and then we'll see about having fun."

"What-EVER" he said while giving me the finger, and with that he took off, leaving me on the porch. I was the only one in jail so there was no reason for them to post a guard yet. I leaned over the railing and looked around. The street was dark and quiet again after the momentary mayhem of the jailbreak.

It was still warm even though the sun had gone down a while ago. The humidity made a haze in the night air you could see around the streetlights. The cicadas had quieted down, all finishing their song at the same time on some unspoken instinctive signal. I could see lights on in most houses. It was a clear night but only the brightest stars could get past the orange glow of the city lights to the east which blotted out the more distant stars. The big dipper was clear and hung over the northern edge of the horizon.

The peaceful street scene was interrupted by two kids sprinting out from a front yard into the middle of the street, chased by another kid that looked like Timbo. They split, one veering to this side of the block and one to the opposite side. Classic escape maneuver, splitting up. Timbo veered after the opposite side kid, and they all disappeared back into the yards and cover, and it was quiet again.

I heard voices coming from alongside the house so went over and leaned over the railing down the driveway. Ant had one of the Dimopoulos kids, presumably caught and now about to join me in jail.

"Hey Kostos! Are you seriously that slow that *this guy* caught you? Did you fall asleep in your spot or something?"

He started laughing, "No, fell out of a tree in back and he tagged me on the ground. Couldn't get my breath" he said.

"Really? You ok now? Also, what the hell is that Ant?"

"Hey, I made sure he was ok first, he's good. It's fair, I didn't make him fall out of the tree."

"Yeah, no it's ok, I'm ok, he got me fair."

Ant walked Kostos to the front porch and then headed back down the driveway, turned into the backyard and I don't know where he went after that. He was probably going to start lurking around trying to pick off anyone who tried to rescue us.

At least now that there were two of us the odds of a rescue were increased, but we wanted to try to spot anyone lurking around jail (like Ant) and call it out, so we took up positions on opposite sides of the porch to increase our field of vision.

I liked Kostos, but we didn't hang out very much. Their family owned the diner that was on the same block as the movie theater downtown, and their father expected them to pitch in and help. They were also pretty active in their church, and between those two responsibilities plus school they didn't have the same amount of free time as the rest of us.

After some discussion, we both decided to make a run for the opposite side of the street when we got sprung, based on nothing other than the fact that both of us had been on this side when we got caught. It seemed like the seekers had focused more on this side, at least from what we had seen, so we felt our odds were better over there.

The conversation turned to hiding places. They lived at the other end of the block so between us we had the landscape pretty well covered, but naturally each was more familiar with our respective ends.

"Back here. See that gap between Ricky's house and the tree line? You can get in there and scoot down along the house and almost the whole yard and then into Mrs. Wild's backyard."

"Back by the garage is where it comes out?"

"Uh huh."

"That's almost the same as by the Pavliks' apartments, you can get all the way through into the back and then behind those garbage cans for a clean shot into the alley."

"Really? That puts you out by Pleasant Street apartments. The manager there is a super a-hole though, right?."

"Oh yeah, Marty the Martian. He's still mad at us still about his truck."

"Marty the Martian? Why? What did you guys do?"

"He has a thing about people from other countries being here, always saying mean things to us and to my mom and dad. He writes letters to the papers about foreigners taking jobs and all kinds of crazy things. Anyway, he was yelling at my dad one time about how his restaurant was bad and my dad asked if he'd ever been there, and Marty said, 'The only way I'll go there is when there's soap on the windows and a for sale sign on the door, just to laugh, and hopefully that day is soon."

"Wow, really? What a jerk, everyone loves your dad's place. When my grandfather visits the first thing he does when he wakes up is go there for some sweet rolls, those things are the best."

I wasn't lying, they were the largest and most frosting covered cinnamon rolls you could get, and probably not the best thing for my diabetic grandfather, but whatever, they were amazing. Kostos' father insisted on all baked goods being made from scratch and fresh and it showed. Even the rolls on the table smelled and tasted better than anything.

"Oh yeah? I'll tell my dad; he'll be glad to hear that. Anyway, when we heard what he said we decided to give him some soap, you know, for the windows. So what we did was put cans of shaving cream - the foamy kind, not the gel kind, very important - into the freezer overnight. Then the next day, when they were frozen solid we used a can opener and cut the bottom of the can off. He drives that pickup truck with the little sliding window in the back of the cab, I don't think it can lock, so we tossed the cans in through that window and once they start defrosting the foam expanded. A lot."

"No way!" I had heard about this but never tried it. "It actually works?"

"Oh yeah it works. It's surprising how much foam is in those little cans." He was grinning.

"That…. that is awesome! Did it fill the truck?"

"No, which was too bad because I really wanted to. Still though, it was a pretty good amount of foam, at least up to the dash."

"How many cans did you use?"

"Like six or seven maybe?"

"So what do you think it would have taken to fill the cab?"

"Probably twice as much. Like twelve cans maybe? That seems like a lot though."

I was still impressed. "I mean yeah, at that point you're kinda just littering in his truck, which I'm not saying he doesn't deserve, but it doesn't send the same message."

"I might have tried it but that's a lot of cans of shaving cream to freeze and carry and open and stuff. I don't know, maybe we should give it another shot," he shrugged, still grinning.

"Wow. Your mom didn't say anything about six or seven cans of shaving cream in the freezer? My mom would have a lot of questions."

"Nah. We have a chest freezer in the basement that we use to store things, she doesn't go in there too much."

"That's awesome. I like that you can use this one any time, not just in winter like the garbage can trick."

"What's that?"

"This one only works when it's freezing or below freezing out. You need a plastic garbage can, it can't be a bucket, it needs to be a bigger container with a flat-ish bottom. Put some plastic wrap in the bottom and make sure there's a couple inches up the sides. Then you pour grape Kool aid into the can and leave it out, so it freezes. Just like a little bit, maybe a quarter inch thick is all you need, don't pour the whole pitcher down there. Anyway, once it's frozen you can use the plastic to lift it out so now you have a frozen sheet of grape Kool aid. Slide it under the gap of any door and then it will defrost. Boom, like you magically spilled on their carpet without opening the door."

"I like it! Have you tried it?

"Not yet."

"Let me know if you do, although we might try it our ourselves."

"Yeah man. Marty sounds like he deserves to have his carpet ruined. If you do, let me know how it goes."

"Deal." Kostos was cool.

"Hey … hey hey look over there. Is that one of ours?"

We could see someone creeping along the porch by the Kaminskis' house.

"Is that a Ghostbusters shirt? I think it's my brother,"

"Maybe, it's hard to tell. Check down the side see if there's anyone hiding there waiting."

We both checked all around as best we could and didn't see anyone, but it didn't matter because Kostos' brother got picked off before he could get to the can by Timbo who came up from the side of Mrs. Wild's house. So now there were three of us in jail, and we were soon joined by two more, led by Ant from the far end of the block.

While adding the other side of the block to the boundaries had succeeded in slowing the game down, it didn't give the runners as much advantage is you would think, especially against such experienced seekers and soon enough we were all in jail except for Ant's brother Andy making him the winner.

"Hey Andy! We got everyone else, you win, you can

come out" his brother yelled. We all sat around waiting for him. "I'll go check down the block, maybe he didn't hear."

We often lost kids playing Kick the Can, so this was nothing out of the ordinary. Some hiding spots were so tucked up in somewhere or far enough away from the can that you couldn't see or hear what was going on, so you had no idea what was happening with the game or if it was over. I don't think any of us had ever tried to fake someone out of a good spot by pretending the game was over, and that would be a despicable thing to do, but technically I think it would have been legal to try, although none of us would.

We were still not alarmed or even bothered when Ant came back a couple minutes later shrugging, "I couldn't find him. Anyone see him while they were out there?"

One complication with the search and recovery of Andy was that we couldn't walk around yelling his name. Because it was night and most of our parents were trying to have a good time without having kids interrupt, if we started making a racket we would all be sent inside, or worse they would make us go watch movies with the little kids.

"C'mon man, are you sure he didn't go inside or something? He's not *that* good," Ricky said.

"I don't think so, unless he got hurt, but we probably would have known about that sooner."

"OK yeah fair. Probably found a good spot and can't hear us. Peaches, lets you, me, and Ant do a quick search mission and see if we can find him, but everyone else stay here so we don't have to send out another mission to find the people who went out to find the person after we find the person. If that makes sense."

It did. My brother, who was Andy's best friend, said, "I'll go with you, I know a lot of his spots, it'll be faster" and that seemed like a good idea so the four of us headed down the driveway towards the alley, and then north, down towards the far end of the block.

"Ant, did you check that little hallway thing between the apartments down there? I've been in there and not heard my mom calling, it's like a reverse echo chamber or something in there."

"Yah, I took a quick look and also that tree that hangs over the garage down there, nothing."

"Hmm…I think he's probably in a garage then, right?"

"Do you guys hear that?"

We all stopped and stood still, quietly listening, in the alley by where the Barlows' garage used to be. All that was left there now was a concrete pad the size of a two-car garage. From behind us we heard what sounded like a cat hissing and growling only deeper.

"What is that? Is it a cat?"

"Maybe … where though? Back there? I don't see it."

"It sounds like it's coming from Wild's," Ant said, his head cocked to one side like a dog, intently listening.

"Let's check it out."

Mrs. Wild's garage had a driveway, so there was no alley access to the garage. We scooted along the Barlow side of the garage, and Ant got to the window and peeked in, hand over his eyes against the glass.

"Oh shhh…. hey, we got a problem." We all crowded around looking in the window. The raccoons, it seems, had struck back.

One of my earliest memories is of being stung by a wasp. I was really little, maybe three or four years old, and was outside standing next to a large hedge. I have my hand out, like I was reaching for something or was trying to grab into the hedge, but there is a large black wasp bouncing off the top of my hand, stinging me. I was terrified. I was so scared I couldn't even talk, couldn't yell out to my mom who was in our yard right behind me. She finally came over, said "Oh my goodness" shooed the wasp off my hand and took me in to put some baking soda and water on it which stopped the stinging. I have never forgotten being so scared I couldn't talk or move or anything, and I have hated wasps ever since.

So when I saw the look on Andy's face, I knew what he was going through. He was up on the long workbench that was in the corner of the garage. There were three large raccoons on the ground between him and the door, and they were not happy: hissing, growling, showing their teeth, and most importantly blocking the exit.

These things just didn't give a damn. I don't know how well racoons can remember people, or carry a grudge, but the earlier Silver Server incident came back to me. They weren't looking scared of people at all right now.

"Hey man … Ricky, do you think these are the ones we got into it with? Across the alley from your house?"

"Does it matter?"

"I don't know. Maybe if we have some kind of connection..."

"We can what, try reasoning with them? You want to talk it out with raccoons? Hey," he said to my brother, "are any of them Bandit?" My brother had named one of the raccoons we had placed under surveillance earlier, but we never could tell which one was Bandit for sure.

"I…it's hard to tell …I don't know…"

Great. Since we used the candle trick we hadn't been there when the fireworks had gone off, but we had certainly spent enough time tracking them and watching them to maybe recognize if they were the same ones. "Are they the same?"

"I don't know, how can you tell?" Ricky was squinting through the glass.

"Maybe their markings, like around the eyes or something? Or the tail, like whales."

"What do you mean like whales?"

"That's how they track whales, they have distinct markings on their tails so they can tell them apart." I had learned this from a National Geographic oceanography book.

"Is that the same though? Whales are mammals. Are racoons mammals?"

"Yah I think so, it should translate."

"*Guys do you need to discuss that right now?*" Ant interrupted the scientific debate we were having.

"Oh, yeah right, sorry Ant."

If I had to guess I would say that the group was using the garage as a nest or nursery or whatever they did in the neighbor's garage before they got kicked out, probably because we had harassed them out of their other spot in that dude's backyard. Andy had gone in to hide and they had seized upon the opportunity for payback, and now here we were in this strange standoff.

"Hey…. heyyyyyy Andy…." Ant was trying to get

his attention without getting too loud. The last thing we needed right now was for adults or even worse Pasha the Coyote to get involved. No luck though. I don't know how long he had been in there with them, but Andy was clearly going through some kind of trauma right now and was not responding. He stayed up on the bench curled up in a sitting position with his arms wrapped around his legs. Probably thinking about how those rabies shots in the stomach were going to hurt.

"Ok, so he's not going to get down with those racoons in there now. Can we get him?"

"Are you saying you want to go *in* there?"

"I think we're going to have to unless we can scare them off. Can we scare them off? What do you guys have? Anything?"

We all did a quick inventory check. While we did have a pretty good number of firecrackers, we didn't think they would be a good solution. We'd used fireworks on the raccoons before and we were unsure of what the effect would be in this situation. For all we knew it would just make them angrier. Maybe as a last last *last* resort.

We had rope/twine/string in decent quantities but couldn't think of a good use for it. We certainly weren't about to try and lasso or trap the things. Even if we did somehow manage to rope one, it didn't feel like that would change the situation much.

We all had pocketknives of various makes and models, but none of us had any delusions of taking a raccoon in hand-to-hand combat. We were running out of ideas.

"We gotta try and flush them out. Where did they get in? The door is shut."

"Let's try opening the door, maybe they'll take an exit if we give them one."

"Yeah, good idea."

"Wait – what happens if they do? We shouldn't all be hanging out right here they might turn around and go back in, let's give them a chance to run. One guy opens the door and the rest of us wait in the alley for a few, right?"

"I'll get the door. You guys get out of here." my brother said. He had guts for sure, and he wasn't about to leave his friend.

"OK. You might have to put a shoulder to it, but it'll go. Me and Ricky got in ok once but it was a while ago. Just a good-sized crack is all you need, ok? And don't stand around once you get it open, just pop it and go."

"Got it. Go."

"We'll let you know when we're in position."

"*Will you go.*"

"Ok, ok, ok, we're going."

We went back around the side of the garage into the alley. None of us felt real good about this arrangement, but we knew there was no arguing with him, and we didn't have a better plan.

"We're ready when you are" Ant hissed around the corner.

We heard a thump. My brother got it open in one so it must not have been stuck too bad, and then … nothing. We stood there in the dark alley, listening for any change or anything coming towards us. Nothing.

"Hey. You ok?" Ant asked.

"Yeah," my brother answered, "it's open, but they aren't coming out."

We went back around the garage so we could see for

ourselves. Now that the door was opened a bit we had a better view of the entire situation, and it was not improving.

"We could put some food by the door." Ant suggested.

"These things aren't stupid, they're not falling for that," said Ricky. He was right.

"We have ropes, can we get to him by swinging over there? Like maybe try and get one over that rafter?" Ant was getting desperate trying to come up with a solution.

"Ok Tarzan, and then what? Now we'll have two people trapped over there."

"Throw rocks until they leave?"

"Does it look like they're leaving? Anyway, that would probably just make them madder, or worse …"

"So…what's left? Go get my dad?"

The problem with getting parents involved was that you never knew if it was going to make things better or worse, and usually it ended up being a combination of both. The situation would be immediately resolved, but then there were questions about what you were doing in there, why did you mess with raccoons, some kind of arbitrary and overly restrictive rules implemented and blah blah blah. You only go there when you are absolutely certain you have exhausted every other option, and you have no expectations of being treated fairly but the problem has gotten so bad that you are willing to risk it.

"Get me out of here guys," Andy had snapped out of the terror paralysis, but I don't know if that was necessarily a good thing because he was starting to panic now. I guess he really had a thing about raccoons, or more likely about rabies shots.

Ricky said, "Hang on man we're working on it. How did you get in?"

"The door," Andy replied. That was not an option at the moment.

"Can you feel any loose boards around you?" Ricky asked. "Maybe we could get you out through the wall into the alley." It wasn't a bad idea. That's how we had gotten in before, maybe we could get lucky.

Andy pushed on the boards around him. "Nah nothing, all nailed tight. Hurry up you guys, I don't like this." He was really scared.

"Look, we can just throw a pack of firecrackers in there and it will scare them off."

"Or it will confirm to them that we are the guys who did it to them before and make them even more angry, and he's still trapped."

Ideas were running short. We were all starting to feel like there were no other options and it was time to get Mr. Kaminski.

"Guys … they're starting to get closer." Andy was right. The raccoons, perhaps having sensed our disarray, were starting to group up and move in. This was not good at all.

My brother said, "You guys move away from that door."

We all thought he was going to take another look or maybe try to signal Andy or something, so we moved to the side. He stepped sideways through the door into the garage, picked up an old shovel that was leaning against the wall with a couple other miscellaneous landscaping tools and swung it around hard, connecting with the side of one of the raccoons sending it tumbling into the opposite wall.

The follow through of that swing had him in position to take another, and he did – another swing that connected with the ass of the second raccoon. This one was too big to get airborne, but it flipped around. Again he had a good follow through and swung the shovel around and down, this time slamming it into the ground right in front of the third and largest raccoon.

Everyone froze in place, even the raccoons. My brother and the third raccoon were staring at each other, waiting to see who was going to make the next move.

"Andy," my brother said in a calm, measured tone, "go for the door. Now." He had them against the opposite wall, leaving a corridor behind him Andy could use to make a break for the door, which he did.

Once he saw Andy make it to the door, he shook the shovel over his head with both hands, threw it in the raccoons' general direction and ran for the door.

"*Close it, close it, close it!*" he was chugging at us as he went through, so me and Ricky pulled it shut. We were shocked. Ant put his arm around his little brother's shoulders "You ok?" He had his hands on his knees and was bent over at the waist like a gassed point guard.

"Yeah. Let's get out of here," Andy said, and we headed back down the driveway towards the front of the block.

We got out front, Ant yelled over to the kids sitting on my porch, "Found him, all good!" and we all stood out front there for a minute. Me and Ricky were looking at my brother.

We all started laughing at the same time. The image of my brother wailing away on those raccoons with a shovel was just too much.

"What? I had to do something, you were all just

standing around coming up with worse and worse ideas. I hope those raccoons are ok, I feel really bad about that. *I'm sorry guys. I'm sorry Bandit if that was you,*" he called back down the driveway. He really had a deep affection for nature and animals, doing what he did must have been difficult for him in more ways than one.

Ricky and I looked at each other for a second, then Ricky put his arm around him and said, "You are a weird guy, but I have never seen anyone do anything like that. Totally awesome."

I agreed, "Yeah that was really brave. And stupid. But mostly brave."

My brother just said, "He's my best friend," and shrugged.

"Yeah, but still, attack with a shovel wasn't even on my list of possibilities,"

"Yeah seriously, thanks man, I owe you one," Ant said.

"That was pretty cool though," Andy said. It seemed like he had gotten over the terror and was calming down. Or the adrenaline was wearing off.

"It was. I don't think I'll forget that for like …ever."

"Neither will those raccoons I bet. Especially that second one you got in the ass, he's going to think of you every time he tries to sit down for the next week."

We weren't up for another round of Kick the Can, and it was getting late anyway so we decided to pack it in for the night. We stood around talking with everyone for a little while longer re-telling the tale, letting my brother re-enact his assault and rescue. Eventually the group broke up and kids started slowly heading home. The street was mostly quiet again, just distant goodbyes and goodnights floating down the block.

15
JAMES BARLOW SUMMONS THE DEVIL

Jake and Elwood?"

"Mmmmm…I don't know. It's just a dark suit and glasses."

"Right, right. E.T. and Elliott?"

"How are you going to do E.T.?"

"You wouldn't have to do the whole body; he was wearing a blanket. So it would be more like a mask and a pear-shaped whatever under a blanket."

"Ehhh…."

"OK then. Johnny and Ponyboy?"

"They're just greasers, no one will get it."

"Han and Luke?"

"We need to find something a little less popular."

"Bo and Luke?"

It was serious business choosing a Halloween costume. You had to try to find the right balance between unique and identifiable, and it had to be something you could make yourself. We didn't do store bought costumes, primarily because they were expensive, especially for something you could only wear one time. Besides, if you bought one there was a good chance someone else would be wearing the same one, and that just wasn't cool. We wanted something different, and memorable. And homemade, which meant we needed a *lot* of lead time.

There was always the chance that things would hit a point where it got too complicated or too far beyond our skills and budget to continue. What happened more often was we would just mess it up and then lose interest so the idea would be scrapped. We had learned to allow for these kinds of things by getting an early start.

It was not uncommon to have Halloween costume discussions in August. My brother occasionally brought ideas to the dinner table for family debate. No one thought it was strange, although to be fair my brother had also brought us conversations on topics such as "Let's get a monkey, I know a guy who can get us one for free," (to which my mom replied, "Well if they're free why not get two?") and "Can we make gunpowder in the garage," so maybe we had a different baseline for what would be considered normal dinner conversations.

That's why we didn't think much of it when we noticed some decorative tombstones on the Barlows' front lawn. After all, it was nearly the end of August, and for us after the Fourth of July the next big holiday was Halloween, and it was one of the best holidays there was, maybe second only to Christmas.

Most people put up outdoor Halloween decorations, and some got pretty elaborate. The year before the Dimopoulos brothers had set up a little haunted house in their garage with a mini-maze and everything. They even had a ghost on a wire they would drop down on people from the rafters, it was cool. Plenty of people went beyond the carved pumpkins and scarecrows and into haunted graveyards, various monsters, and life-sized creatures. Maybe the Barlows were just getting a head start. Besides, there was nothing else to do, why not?

It had been pretty quiet around the neighborhood after the Fourth of July. We hadn't seen James Barlow at all really after the garage fire, which was fine with us because he hadn't been messing with any of us. Maybe he got blamed for it. Maybe he did it. We were being left alone so whatever the reason was we didn't care.

Ricky and I were playing catch out front across the yards. Official league baseball was over for the year, so we didn't have practices or games or anything where we had to be. It was the winding down of another summer and we were going to enjoy it before we had to be back in school in a few weeks.

I put a little too much on a high toss and it went over Ricky's head, bouncing and rolling down into the Barlows' yard where it stopped. He jogged down to grab the ball among the wooden tombstones, then stopped and looked for a second before coming back. He was shaking his head.

"What?"

"One of them had a name on it." We had never looked closely at them before now.

"Anyone we know?"

"Do you know a Randy Roadees? Or is it Roads? However you say it."

"Who? No."

"Me either."

"Sounds made up. It's probably some movie character like Jason Vorhees or Indiana Jones."

"Maybe, I dunno." Ricky shrugged and tossed the ball back to me.

We went back to playing catch and didn't think much of it, and it was forgotten by the end of the day for sure. It wasn't until later that week that I found out who "Randy Roads" was.

I was over at Rob Kelton's checking out his new guitar, a black Fender Stratocaster. No amp, but he had somehow rigged his stereo to allow him to plug into it, and it sounded pretty good. "I Love Rock and Roll" and "Eye of the Tiger" were getting heavy radio play at the time, and I was already a fan of Van Halen thanks to the release of *1984*, so I felt I was pretty familiar with the sounds of heavy guitar. I had no idea how deep the rabbit hole I was about to fall down was.

"What's with the black scarf?" Rob had a thin black scarf tied around the headstock of the Strat.

"Just want to be like my hero Jimi Hendrix."

"Who?"

"Jimi Hendrix? You don't know who Jimi Hendrix is?"

"No, sorry."

"That guy," he was pointing to a poster of Jimi on his wall, a picture taken from Monterey Pop where he lit his guitar on fire. "Here, listen to this," he put on *Smash Hits* and played along with "Red House." I was totally blown away. I had no idea you could make so many different sounds with a guitar like Jimi did, always thought of it as more of a rhythm-solo-rhythm format so I was eager to hear more. This Jimi guy was like

Eddie Van Halen from Mars, maybe there were others who played like him.

"Who's that? Does he play like Jimi Hendrix too?" I was pointing at a poster of a white guy with a polka dot "v" shaped guitar. He looked a lot like Ricky actually, if Ricky was older and had longer hair.

"No. That's Randy Rhoads, he was in Quiet Riot and then he was Ozzy Osbourne's guitar player." The name rang a bell, but I couldn't remember why.

"What does he sound like?"

"Well, he used to sound like this, but he died," Rob said, dropping the needle on "Crazy Train" from *Blizzard of Oz*, "Plane crash earlier this year." I had seen so many Ozzy t-shirts, but I had never actually listened to the music. It was great.

All the information I was getting combined with all the awesome music was a bit too much for my brain to handle all at once. I was totally hooked on Jimi Hendrix and Ozzy Osbourne/Randy Rhoads, and I hung out with Rob for the afternoon letting him play all this different stuff I had never heard before like Motorhead and Iron Maiden, eventually leaving his house a new heavy metal fan, so I had my mind on other things and didn't make the connection until later.

We were walking to 7-11, bouncing these little superballs we had found in a bowl at the toy store. They were like a nickel a piece, so we bought the whole bowl's worth of them and now we were always whipping them around. They were super bouncy but also super cheaply made and would start to crack and crumble after a bit of use and abuse.

Ricky bounced his off one of the fake headstones and said, "Sorry Randy Whoever-you-are."

"Rhoads. Wait I know who he is now! He was a guitar player for Ozzy Osbourne, he died in a plane crash earlier this year."

"Really? Huh. Yeah, James is a big Ozzy fan, he's got that *Diary of a Madman* shirt he's always wearing. I guess it makes sense." James Barlow and Ozzy Osbourne seemed a natural match for each other.

On the way back, drinking Big Gulps, we stopped to talk with Amy Barlow who was sitting on their front steps.

"Hey. What's this all about anyway?"

"Oh, James has this all for Randy. He's really upset. He's been really upset since the plane crash happened," Amy told us.

"Really?" I was having a hard time visualizing James Barlow in such a state.

"Yeah, keeps saying stuff about him. He spends a lot of time in his room. You should see it, all covered in Randy Rhoads posters. I think maybe that's part of why he started out here, he's out of space inside."

"Wow. Saying stuff like what?"

"Just stuff. Like he just wishes he could hear him one more time, he wishes he could have told him, or wants to tell him, stuff like that. Some other stuff... I don't want to get into it. He took my diary and some other things and I'm afraid he won't give it back if I say anything ... so anyway, that's why this is on the lawn, it's like a memorial thing. I don't know really. I like to listen to the radio, not heavy metal, so I don't know much about it."

"So is he going to leave this all up here like ... forever?" Ricky asked. I could see he was getting a little weirded out by this.

"I don't think so. I don't know." she shrugged. "He really liked him."

"I liked Randy too," I said, "he could really play."

She just looked at me with an expression that was somewhere between disbelief and curiosity. I don't know if she was trying to figure out if I was serious, or wanted to say something else, or if she just thought I was an idiot and couldn't hide it. Whatever, if you didn't like metal you probably thought that about everyone who did, so I brushed it off. We said our goodbyes and Ricky and I headed for his deck in back.

"That was … weird." Ricky said thoughtfully.

"Yeah man. I wonder what James is up to. What do you think she meant by 'a memorial thing'?" I was intrigued.

"Who knows. It'll probably end up nothing like all his other big stunts. Just like his dad. Let's go, I want to play River Raid." He had another new game for Atari, and we were still in that "just got a new game" life consuming phase of it. Plus, it was really hot out and sitting in a little air conditioning sounded good right now, so that was the end of the discussion.

Two nights later, we were in Ricky's family room playing River Raid again. I was sleeping over, so we could sit up all night playing Atari – mostly River Raid, but we also had Pitfall (new) and a couple others we were trying to beat. I liked sleeping over at Ricky's. Besides the Atari, they had air conditioning, and we did not. Also, we slept on the big sectional in the family room that was right next to the kitchen, so that meant easy access to unlimited snacks and soda. Sleepovers at Ricky's didn't happen a lot because his stepmom was pretty unstable temperament-wise, and it wasn't always a good situation to be in. Or Ricky would be grounded and couldn't have friends over.

I don't know specifically what the issue or issues were, we never talked about it, but my bedroom window faced their back door (it was on the side of the house towards the rear) which was in their kitchen, and I could hear her screaming at him when she got going. Sometimes it got bad. She had him against a wall one time screaming right in his face, I could see through the door. Like I said, we never talked about it, but he knew I knew.

This was how Ricky got the Atari in the first place, a combination of his stepmom's guilt and payment for silence to his father I think. I knew whenever there was a bad fight because he had a new game. It seemed like he was getting a lot of new games lately.

"Peaches, go grab some Cokes out of the fridge, will ya? I swear this level is adapting to me or something. Every time I get close to that bridge these missiles come out of nowhere and pin me in the corner. Dammit!" he cursed as he got blown up again by the missiles in the corner.

As I went past the sliding deck doors I happened to look out and see light and movement in the Barlows' backyard. It looked like someone was back there with a flashlight. I couldn't really see what they were doing. At the moment it looked like they had set the flashlight down and were doing something on the ground, but I couldn't make out what.

"Hey … hey man someone's in the Barlows' back yard with a flashlight."

"Cops?"

"I don't think so. Check it out."

"Hold on, I have one life left lemme take one last run at this... *Dammit!* Ok, what are we looking at here?"

"Back there, see?"

Just to the left of the big tree in their back yard we could see someone moving around in silhouette thanks to a flashlight on the ground.

"Too small for an adult. What's going on back there?"

"Maybe we should get a closer look."

Ricky put on his shoes, and we slipped out the sliding deck door, carefully closing it so it wouldn't thump or lock. We went out while I was sleeping over plenty of times. Ricky's stepmom usually steered clear of us while I was there, so we weren't worried about her noticing we were gone. Also, and this is what we figured we would say if we did get caught, we were just going out on the deck, so *technically* not leaving the house. Of course, we did in fact leave the deck, but we had the "heard a noise/thought an animal was hurt" excuse lined up. It was the easiest sneaking out I've ever done, no climbing out windows or sneaking past parents' bedroom doors or anything like that.

It was still hot and muggy even though it was past midnight. We tried to stay low on the deck, and keep in the shadows, working our way towards the back edge so we could look out across the yards into the Barlows.

"I think that's James."

"Yeah, I think so too. Is he looking for something?"

"Hard to tell from over here. Let's try to get a better angle."

"Can you see if Pasha is out?"

"She's not, we would have heard her barking at rats or rabbits or ghosts or whatever ...c'mon let's go, we can hop the fence back over there quietly."

We carefully climbed onto the outside of the deck railing, edged along until we were next to one of the pine trees on the property line and used it to step onto and then over the fence, gently hopping down into Mrs. Wild's back yard, and got next to the back of her house, peeking around the corner.

We had closed the distance by half, but we still couldn't quite figure out what James was doing. Now that we were closer, we could hear him talking but we weren't close enough to hear what he was saying. This was starting to get very strange.

"What's going on?"

"I don't know. Doesn't seem like he's looking for something though, he's staying in one spot and not sweeping that flashlight. Wait... is that a shovel? Is he digging?"

"No, filling in, look…" James had his back to us but was using a small shovel to backfill a shallow hole off to the yard-side of the tree. He used the back of the shovel to pat down the earth and then moved what looked like a stainless-steel mixing bowl on to the top of it. I couldn't see what he put into it, but it was some items off the ground and something from his pocket. I did see what I recognized as a bottle of lighter fluid, which he used to hose down the contents of the bowl and then dropped in a match.

He was kneeling in front of it with his head down, still talking but we couldn't hear what he was saying and didn't want to risk getting closer.

"Dude … what the ….?"

"I don't know. Let's just hang here and watch what happens."

Nothing happened. James knelt there for a little bit but eventually the fire went out, James stood up, shook the ashes out of the bowl onto the fresh dirt it had been sitting on and then went up the back stairs into his house.

I gave the thumb over my shoulder to Ricky, and he nodded. We headed back across the yard, but before we got to the fence Ricky grabbed my wrist.

"Wait, I want to go over there and look. Real quick, just wait for me here."

I hated it when he did this. There's always a moment when you are doing something risky where you stop being as confident that you won't get caught. Like if you know you have 45 minutes to get clear, it's usually around minute 37 I start getting nervous. This was also usually when Ricky would want to do one more thing or stay for one more minute. He would push it right up to the point of no return sometimes. I think everyone has an appetite for risk, but his was greater than mine.

"Ok but be fast, seriously."

He worked his way around the edge of the house and then out into the yard where I lost him in the overgrowth and dark. I was alone in the driveway, dealing with The Fear.

The Fear is very real, and it tries to get to you in moments like this. Every memory of every time you got caught, every bad premonition, every snap of a twig or rustle from the bushes all start to build into an unnerving and relentless wave of negative that can make you panic, lose confidence, and in general do something stupid that actually will get you caught, or worse. I could always tell when it was coming. My heart would start pounding, mouth went dry, thoughts started racing, and there was an overwhelming desire to be somewhere else. Somewhere "safe." I'm not saying that everything we did was do-or-die, and this situation certainly wasn't, but even when you were doing something mildly out of bounds you had to keep your head and be smart, and I had learned the hard way that The Fear was not something to be treated lightly.

I heard Ricky coming back around the house after what felt like twenty minutes but was actually more like three, and he made the OK sign with his fingers and pointed at his house. I nodded and we headed back up the fence, over the railing and in through the deck door.

"Did you get close? What was over there?"

"I dunno man. I couldn't see anything really, just some ashes and a pile of dirt where he filled in that hole. It's too dark, we'll have to try and sneak a peek tomorrow during the day."

"Ok. Let's play Pitfall, all that River Raid is making it hard to focus my eyes and it feels like everything is scrolling down..."

In the morning I went home to shower, eat, change clothes, and let my mom know I was still alive and in the area. She was heading out, so I was left in charge of my brother. This was not a big deal, and also a regular occurrence, because my mom was pursuing a master's degree and taking classes during the summer when she wasn't teaching. My brother could handle himself, the only time he ever needed me when our parents weren't around were to get a second opinion on if a cut needed stitches, or to use the stove. I didn't even know if he was home and didn't bother checking if he was before I took off. My mom left a note on the table for him, so I just wrote: "Out and about, holler if you need me,

Peaches" underneath her message, which was far more detailed.

Since Ricky had to go to family counseling with his stepmom and wouldn't be back until this afternoon, I figured one of us should try to check out the Barlows' back yard, and no time like the present. It was one of those overcast days that was so humid and hot you knew it was going to thunderstorm at some point, so I wanted to get a look before the rain washed anything interesting away.

I went out the back door, hopped the fence, cut through Ricky's yard, hopped the fence into Mrs. Wild's yard and then worked my way through the path we had worn down through the overgrown grass and bushes until I was right behind the tree in the Barlows' back yard. I sat there for a couple minutes, just listening and making sure no one was around. When I was satisfied the coast was clear I edged around the alley side of the tree, keeping it between me and the Barlows' house, figuring it would give me better cover that way if anyone came out or provide a line for my escape in case they let Pasha the Coyote out.

As I came around the side of the tree and stepped into the yard, I could see the fresh dirt pile, but there was more. The grass was long gone from Pasha putting in some work back there, it was just dirt and occasional tufts of grass. The mound was in the center of an inverted triangle that had been scraped into the ground, like a little trench. At each of the triangle's points was a different shape or symbol. I didn't recognize any of them. At the bottom there was small pile of what looked like bones. If I had to guess I would say they were chicken leg bones left over from a barbeque.

I felt fear well up from my stomach to my chest, like when you are running up the basement stairs and you're afraid to look back because it feels like something is going to grab your ankle the second you get the light switch. A wave of panic hit me hard, and I turned and booked it as fast as I could, not stopping until I got back to my own back yard, where I immediately fell over the fence trying to jump it and landed in my mom's flower garden, smashing a few violets and spraying dirt all over the sidewalk.

Then I felt fine. I sat there almost laughing out loud. I got The Fear from James Barlow's half assed voodoo shrine or whatever it was. *What was my damage* as my brother would say. I grabbed the hose and sprayed down the sidewalk and flower bed to cover up the destruction while trying to piece together what had just happened. I had noticed recently that I would sometimes get The Fear once in a while for no reason at all or in situations where I didn't have anything to be afraid of, and this could have just been one of those times. I was pretty sure it was just me freaking myself out, and I was probably more scared about getting caught by James back there than anything else because I didn't have a lot of belief in the occult or stuff like that.

The distinction between superstition and supernatural was clear for me. I wouldn't consider myself more or less superstitious than any other kid in the neighborhood. We all played baseball and embraced all the lore and rituals that came with the game, and it extended to other things as well. There was a whole list of well-known behaviors that were supposedly bad luck, and we carefully avoided them. No hats on the bed, no three on a match, step on a crack break your mother's back. There was other stuff, too. I wouldn't say "Bloody Mary" into a mirror three times and neither would anyone I knew.

To me, the supernatural was mostly something that happened in movies and on TV. I will admit to being superstitious, but as far as believing in ghosts and demons and all that, I had a hard time with buying it beyond the usual urban legends and neighborhood folklore. I hadn't had any experiences I would consider supernatural, or at least nothing I couldn't attribute to possibilities that were more rational, so there was nothing I could personally relate to. I think it was the whole lack of tangible evidence or credible witnesses that made it tough for me to accept at face value. So many stories were of the "happened to a friend of a friend of a friend" variety it just made me incredulous about all of it because it was always the same thing.

I finished hosing down the yard with more questions than I had answers for, so I decided that what I needed was more information. I went inside, brushed my teeth, yelled "I'm going to the library," into an apparently empty house, added another note to my note on my mom's note to my brother that I was going to the library, and then hopped on my bike.

The sky was starting to look more ominous, especially to the west which was turning a darker greenish gray color. I knew I would be ok getting to the library, it wasn't that far, but getting home might be an issue. Worst case I could just hang out at the library until the storm passed, which wasn't a big deal. I had plenty to look up.

I locked my bike up at the end of the bike rack out

front and headed straight up to the second floor, non-fiction and reference. I was such a regular that I only needed the card catalog for specific books or authors at this point, I knew where everything was by subject and section. The problem was I wasn't exactly sure what the subject was here, or where to start. Religion maybe? That seemed like a good enough place to begin looking so I headed down the rows until I found the section I was looking for.

Paganism, wicca, witchcraft, voodoo … I found a few of books that seemed possibly helpful, but also noticed several gaps in the shelf where other people had taken out books, and this made me feel like I was maybe missing out on the good stuff, but I was able to make do with what was there.

It was still overcast, but there were puddles on the ground, and it smelled like rain when I got back outside. I had been in there for a couple hours and hadn't noticed what was apparently a pretty good storm judging by the amount of water in the streets I had to avoid as I rode home. I put my bike in the garage, hopped the fence, and went up the stairs to Ricky's deck to see if he was home yet.

I could see through the deck doors he was playing Q*bert. Another new game. Not sure what happened at family counseling, but this was the third new game in a month whatever that meant. I let myself in and sat down on the couch.

"Anyone else home?"

"Yeah, my stepmom is upstairs."

"Can you go out?"

"Yeah yeah, sure, let me finish this game and then let's go."

Ten minutes and four "dammits" later (one loud enough to get a "Ricky! *Language!*" from upstairs) we were out on the deck. I told Ricky about what I had found over in the Barlows' yard. He wanted to go see for himself, so we headed around the front and down Mrs. Wild's driveway. Everything was still wet, and we didn't feel like getting soaked cutting through bushes and weeds until we had to.

There was nothing to see. A slight mound in muddy ground and a couple random chicken leg bones was all that was left. I guess the rain had washed it away like I thought it might. It didn't feel any different over here now either.

"I don't know, Peaches. When I was over here last night I don't think I saw any of that. Not saying it wasn't here, just that I didn't see anything like that. It was pretty dark. Are you sure?"

"Yeah, I'm sure. There's more though, let's get out of here and I'll tell you." We sat down on my front porch, and I told him about what I had found in the library.

"So James Barlow is trying to be a witch? Or…what? I don't know man, for all we know he was just recreating cover art you could find on like 20 different metal bands records. I mean, Led Zeppelin 4 isn't technically even named anything it's just those four weird symbols, that whole scene is into all that stuff."

"Ok, so first of all, Led Zeppelin is not heavy metal. Iron Maiden, Judas Priest, Motorhead, that's metal. Led Zeppelin, Jimi Hendrix, Cream, not metal."

"What about Van Halen?"

"I think Van Halen would be more in the 'hard rock' category, maybe Quiet Riot too, kind of a gray area there

I guess. Not enough blood and leather for heavy metal but the guitars are too loud for pop. Look, can we get back to the main subject?"

"Hey, you're the one who got all particular about it. Anyway, so you think James is doing some voodoo things in his back yard because why …?"

"That's what's bothering me. I don't know why. The only information we have is that it might have something to do with Randy Rhoads, but who knows. This is James Barlow we're talking about, maybe he got tired of throwing bricks and breaking stuff and punching people and is moving into different ways to be a jerk."

"You didn't say that though. You didn't find anything at the library that would make me think he was doing that."

"Well, that's been bothering me too. That's the thing, I didn't find anything specific at the library but there were a bunch of books checked out so maybe I couldn't figure out what's going on because what I needed isn't there. Maybe someone else is using those books. Like maybe James."

This made Ricky laugh, "The only way I can imagine James going into a library is with a gas can and a lighter. I think you're imagining things, but I guess he is being kinda weird, first with the tombstones on the front lawn and now this."

"Yeah. Maybe it is nothing. I mean, you're right about the heavy metal album cover thing, it could just be that."

The next couple days were unremarkable. We were busy building and testing a new jump ramp for the bikes in Kaminski's yard so we were in a spot where we could see if there was anything happening in Barlows' back yard, but it was quiet. Not much activity at their house at all, except for Pasha howling at the moon at night.

It was morning, and I was lying in my bed just thinking when Ricky's head popped into my bedroom window. "Peaches! Hey! You up?" he hissed through the screen. It was an easy hop and pull up for him to be able to get his head up to my first-floor bedroom window.

"Hey. Yeah, I'm up."

"Can you come out? Like now?" he sounded a little urgent.

"Yeah, let me get dressed, be there in five."

Six minutes later I was walking up his driveway in bright sunshine, eating a Pop Tart. He was sitting on his back steps.

"Last night I was playing Pitfall, new high score by the way, and saw someone out in the Barlows' yard when I went to the fridge. My dad was still up so I couldn't go over there and look but I'm pretty sure it was James again; we need to go check it out."

I shoved the rest of the Pop Tart into my mouth and nodded, pointing to the spot where we usually hopped the fence from the deck into Mrs. Wild's yard.

"Nah, let's go around, my stepmom is still home, if she goes into the kitchen she could see."

We walked around the front of the house, then down Mrs. Wild's driveway and cut along the back of the house until we were behind the tree on the property line. I had done this hundreds of times, probably thousands, but for whatever reason I was feeling more nervous about being there right now than I had ever been. I could feel my heart rate in my chest. I had Ricky with me this time though, and that calmed me down a bit.

"There, look," I whispered to Ricky.

This time, on the spot where there had been a mound of dirt was a mound of stones. Again, in an inverted triangle that had been scratched into the dirt, and there was a symbol and a rock at each corner this time. This was getting interesting, and now it felt more interesting than scary. My nerves started to ease up.

"Maybe Amy's hamster died, and they decided to go with a crypt instead of in-ground burial," Ricky said sarcastically.

"Only one way to find out."

Ricky grabbed a medium-sized stick off the ground, got as close as he could and poked the stone pile.

"Ew. Definitely something, but not hamster. I think those are feathers?"

I peered over his shoulder. It was really hard to identify anything that was inside the stone pile because it had clearly been torched, but it did look like there were some feathers, or remains of feathers, and possibly some small bones, plus some charred cloth in among the rocks.

"Maybe Amy had a pet bird that kicked it? It looks small whatever it was."

"Let's go." I said as I tugged on his shirt. I had been feeling a little nervous, but not like the other day. I didn't want to get caught back there, but I wasn't totally freaking out either. We cut back around the rear of the house and back out front.

"That was different."

It was different. It seemed sad. Pathetic. I can't explain why, but maybe after doing a little research and getting a second look I just couldn't be scared of it. In fact, I felt kinda guilty we had messed up what was possibly a pet's gravesite, like maybe it was someone's business we shouldn't have been around.

"You feel ok?" I asked him.

"Yeah, fine. I don't eat Pop Tarts, maybe you shouldn't have pounded that one down."

"No I mean, you didn't feel weird being back there?" I was still curious about why I had panicked back there by myself the other day.

"No."

"Not scared?"

"What? No, why would I be, there's no one around. Something up?"

"Nothing, never mind. Let's go somewhere more private," and we headed back to his garage so we could sit in the Mustang and talk.

"OK, so back up little. What exactly did you see last night?" I said from the passenger seat. Ricky had the driver's seat, as usual.

"Same as before, he was out there in the dark, had a flashlight on the ground. I couldn't see much because it was dark, and he had his back to me, so he was blocking my view. Then he went back inside. I don't know how long he was out there before I noticed."

"So you didn't see him lighting it?"

"No. Like I said, I don't know how long he was out there. Or if he came back out later. I didn't hang around waiting, I saw him go in and figured that was it."

"This is so weird, even for him."

"He's pretty weird."

"Fair. I don't know. I don't like it, but at the same time I don't know why or even have a good idea of what he's doing, if anything. But I think we can agree that it's more than just some heavy metal wannabe a wizard crap, he's trying to do…I don't know. Something."

There wasn't really anything else to discuss because there wasn't anything else we could do really. All we knew was that James Barlow was possibly performing some kind of ritual, and we didn't know the purpose. Or even how long it had been going on for. We didn't like it, but at the same time it still seemed a little ridiculous.

It seemed even more ridiculous the next day when we walked past their house on the way to 7-11. The display in front of the house had been expanded, there were now several small rock piles in the shape of graves in front of the fake headstones. There was what looked like an old kids' dresser that had been turned into some kind of altar or display. It was spray painted flat black (James did have some skills with a spray paint can) and there was a plastic skull in the center, with a bunch of those votive candles in jars and some plastic roses. Hanging from the front of the house next to the window that was James's bedroom was an upside down cross.

"Tasteful," Ricky snorted. "Whoa, Look at *that*!" Ricky was pointing at the cross.

"I see it. I wonder when he did all this. It wasn't here yesterday, right?

"Definitely not. What is this guy doing, creating an Ozzy poster in real life?"

"Could be. Let's go, we don't want him seeing us hanging around out here," and we continued on our way. Ricky was talking about some girl, but I was only half paying attention. I was trying to work through what James was doing and it didn't make any sense, which was frustrating because it seemed like there was enough information there for me to figure it out, and I just couldn't put it together. It was like he had pulled bits and pieces and symbols and images from a few different sources and was putting it all together intentionally, but what the purpose of all of it was I couldn't figure out. All we knew was that it had something to do with Randy Rhoads.

"Hey, do you think he's trying to contact Randy Rhoads in the afterlife? Like those séance people on "Believe it Or Not?" I snorted. We tended to end up on the "…Or Not," side of that show when we watched it.

"Maybe. Seems a little ambitious, I think he's just trying to make like a heavy metal memorial for him or something like that. It's so half-assed."

This was a good point. It was half-assed, really half-assed. Like the haunted house me and my brother built in our basement when we were younger that was just a bunch of rigged-up whatever that we had and thought we could make scary. Honestly, the fun was more in building it than in the final product, and that may have been the case with the Barlows' front yard. Maybe he was just throwing out whatever he happened to think of whenever he thought of it.

The upside down cross made more sense in this context. In reality it wasn't Satanic at all, but he thought it was heavy metal so up it went. It was like we were watching James Barlow express himself through lawn art, and the further it went the more we thought it was funny. Even my dad asked at dinner, "Anyone know what is happening with the Barlows? Quite a display they got over there. Getting a great head start for Halloween don't ya think?" and laughing.

Amy was out the next morning, so Ricky and I went down to see what was new. She did not look like she was enjoying the decorations as much as we were.

"Well this is really…. something, huh Amy? Are you going to do a little spell casting too?" Ricky was kind of teasing. He knew Amy had a crush on him (most of the girls in the neighborhood did) so he was also flirting a little too.

Amy was not amused. "I hate this. Bad things are happening. Ever since he hung that upside-down cross up. The vegetable drawer in the fridge broke and everything spilled out, Pasha got sick from eating something and had to get her stomach pumped, me and Kelly both got locked in the bathroom by something but then when we finally got the door open nothing was there and there was no one else home, and the light in the dining room keeps going on and off randomly. It's all because of this I know it is."

"You think so? I mean, those could just be coincidence, right? Sometimes things just happen," I said, not wanting to point out that all of those incidents probably had perfectly reasonable explanations, especially for a family that lived pretty hard and did not seem so interested in preventive home maintenance.

"It all started happening after he put that cross up. It's not funny! Something bad is going to happen you guys, I know it." Ricky was smirking, and I was biting the inside of my cheeks to stop a smile. This was too much. What was next, a demonic clogged toilet? Did this entity only have the power to cause minor household inconveniences?

At the same time, I felt bad for her. I liked Amy, she was a good person and I always felt like it was some kind of cosmic error that she had ended up with that bunch. She was clearly upset and a little scared, although if you had to live with James Barlow, I suppose that would be a semi-normal state to exist in. It kinda made me mad. Why did this guy think it was ok to mess with people so badly? Especially his own family? It seemed like nothing ever happened to him, or if it did, he didn't care it and it did nothing to deter him from whatever stupid mean thing he was going to do next.

We couldn't just leave her like that, so I told her about protective circles, which I had read about when I was looking up all this witchcraft stuff in the library and told her how to make one. At least I might have, admittedly I was out of my element with this. Also not helping was that there was quite a lot of "it's up to you" and "open to interpretation/intention" with this kind of magic (according to the books), so I kinda did my best to cover the bases with her. I think she felt better. At least she felt like she could do something, which was better than before.

"I think we've been coming at this from the wrong direction," Ricky said as we were walking back to my house.

"How's that?"

"Well… I have an idea, maybe a good one…"

I liked Ricky a lot. He was my best friend and practically my second brother. He had excellent situational awareness and could improvise solutions really well, but I would never consider him a deep thinker. I don't think he would be mad if I told him that either. However, the idea he had was so amazing, so genius I have to give it to him. It was so stupid and risky and involved equipment and all that, it was perfect for us. I can't believe I didn't think of it myself.

First we needed to go to Deacon's for some supplies, so we hopped on our bikes and headed for the mall.

Once we were properly geared up, and I had a new marked deck (unrelated, I couldn't help myself sometimes) we headed back to Ricky's garage to start working on the logistics. There were quite a lot of variables in this scenario, but one thing we were sure of - we needed to be ready to make it happen soon. James was clearly escalating whatever it was he was doing, and we would miss our opportunity if we didn't get everything set up and ready to go by the next time he was out performing rituals in his back yard.

Much like the remote bottle rocket launching operation, this plan had several moving pieces and we quickly realized we were one set of hands short, so we needed to get another person. We briefly thought of Amy Barlow, but then decided it would be best for her to not have any knowledge or involvement. Ant, though - he lived right next door to them, hated James as much as we did, could keep a secret and his dad had some tools we might need, so we decided to recruit him.

He was in his back yard switching out the crank on his bike, so we helped him press out bearings and stuff while we told him what we had in mind after making him swear to keep it between us.

"And you guys think this will work? You know we're probably going to get our asses kicked." Ant was not as enthusiastic about it as we were.

"No, we're not. Even if he does figure it out, I'm the only one who's really going to be at risk in the moment and I've gotten bigger since last time we had a fight, and I'm in wrestling, I can handle it now," Ricky said. This was true, he did have a "growth spurt" as my mom would say and between last summer and now had added a couple inches in height (and reach) and a couple pounds of muscle, plus he had taken up wrestling which he was planning to pursue next year at school and was actually kinda good.

"I don't even care anymore. He's not going to have those older guys with him and if there's three of us, screw it," I said. I meant it. I was tired of this guy always having some kind of advantage.

"Ah… well, since I have to see how this plays out now, I guess I'm in." Ant sighed.

"My man! I knew you would. Alright, here's what we need to do," Ricky said, and we got to work. Like nearly every other scheme we came up with, it turned out to be a lot more work than we thought. Stringing the invisible wires in particular turned out to be much more challenging, it was difficult to disguise what we were actually doing and not draw attention to ourselves throwing a rock with string tied around it over tree branches.

"Are you sure hanging these up here is going to be a good idea?" I was still remembering the feeling of being an almost-arsonist, so I wanted to be sure it didn't happen again and wanted to avoid assault and battery.

"It should be fine; it will be out in the air and away from where he is going to be. Probably."

"How strong do you think that wire is though?"

"I don't know … It's good enough, stop worrying about it."

"Hey man, I'm all for a giving him a good scare but I don't want to hurt the guy. Well … I don't want to *seriously* hurt the guy, you know what I mean. This is a little risky don't you think?"

"Do you think he was worried about your personal safety when he threw that quarter stick at you on the Fourth?" My moral dilemma was interrupted by a voice from the other side of the yard.

"Guys .. hey, over here check it out, I found this in the garage, it should work perfect," Ant was calling to us.

We were making pretty good progress working together, and so far the only person who even knew we were doing anything was Mr. Kaminski, but that's just because we were mostly in his backyard. I doubt he knew exactly what we were putting together and even if he did, we weren't all that worried about him because he just did not care about anything. He didn't seem to be paying any attention to us most of the time, and now was not an exception.

Two days later we were all set. It took a little longer than we had hoped because we had to keep it casual to avoid suspicion, but from what we could tell James hadn't been back to his little ritual spot since the last time Ricky saw him. All we had to do now was wait.

It was Friday night when I heard Ricky say "Hey. Peaches. He's out, let's go" through the screen of my bedroom window. Since my bedroom had the unfortunate circumstances of being located on the same side of the house as my parents' room, and their window, I had learned that going out my window was not the best option for sneaking out. Instead, I went downstairs to the basement and crawled out the laundry room window, which was on the driveway side of the house and also the farthest point from my parents, so I didn't have to worry too much about making noise. I met Ricky on the side of his house.

We slipped into Mrs. Wild's backyard and sure enough, there was someone out in the Barlows' backyard with a flashlight, this time with one of those candles-in-a-jar burning, too. I got to my spot, and Ricky tapped me on the shoulder and then headed off down the driveway towards the front of the house, where he would get Ant and then come back to his position here with me, all according to the plan.

Each of us had a critical part, and we had to execute to perfection, and all our gear needed to function as expected. We had a floating ghost that we had made out of some grim reaper costume cloak thing we got cheap at Deacons, tied to the invisible wire, also from Deacons. We also had some line on the trees, going down to a central rope, so I could dramatically shake and sway them. This was my job, to raise the ghost and shake the trees.

For Ant, he had to get in his garage and man the sound system, which was a set of disassembled walkie talkies with the talk button up, so they were like remote speakers. We had one of these wired up by the tree, as well as a couple strategically stashed in different bushes and shrubs around the yard to provide a full panoramic sound experience. He was going to use his boom box to play a tape I had made with creepy sound effects. All Ant had to do was hit "play" and hold the walkie-talkie in front of the box when we gave him the sign, which was three flicks of my low-vis red-lens flashlight. I would be shielded from James behind the big tree, and we had set up a periscope (also from Deacon's) out the side window of his garage to give him a view of the action without having to go out there.

Ricky probably had the most dangerous job, but he was the tallest out of all of us so there was no other choice. Plus, he wanted to do it. Ricky was dressed in all black, had a white expressionless mask and a "heavy metal hair" wig, also from Deacons. He had to come from behind the tree and walk towards James as if he had left Hell in search of someone to bring back with him.

We were expecting James to run if he was scared enough and fooled enough. If he did not run and stood his ground then it was Ricky and I who were going to have to deal with it, and there was no way to predict how angry or violent it could get. Ricky was OK with this, but if it got to that point, it meant pretty much everything had gone wrong, and I don't think I was as OK with that as he was, but I tried not to worry about it.

This was the most ambitious undertaking we had ever attempted, and it was putting to the test all our skills. We had tried to build in redundancies and contingency options because, as the saying goes, no plan survives first contact intact. Most of our plans didn't survive second, third or any other contact either, and typically the more complex the pieces were, and the more we had to rely on hope, the riskier it got. This plan was complex, and hope was the glue that was holding it all together.

From where I was crouched, I could see James was still doing whatever he was doing at his little rockpile shrine on the other side of the big tree in his backyard. Ricky was back, presumably no issues getting Ant into place, ready to come out once I started shaking the trees and dropped the ghost from above us. Ant of course was in his garage, ready with the sound. He was just waiting for my signal.

I had the flashlight clipped to my belt, and I was trying to hold onto the wire and rope in one hand and get the flashlight with my other hand. It was similar to those military ones, "L" shaped but had lights on both ends. The slider went up and down for different lights, one a regular flashlight, one a low-level red light, and you could press the button for pulse, like if you were trying to use morse code.

I was trying to get around the side of the tree to get a good angle and give Ant the signal with the light, but the wire and rope were hard to hold onto, and I guess I was more focused on them because when I flipped up the flashlight to give the signal it was already on, not the red lens but bright light shining out over the yard, partially catching James in the edge of the beam. Ricky, who was on my left, drew in a breath and said," *Peaches what are you doing, kill it, turn off the light.*"

We were completely exposed. James got up from what he was doing, following the light back to its source which was me and Ricky, Ricky in the wig and black getup, me with the light in one hand and rope and stuff in the other.

We just stood there. There was nothing else to do. I couldn't think of anything to do, and besides, I was too terrified. He looked right at us, and I saw recognition tense his face into a grimace. Whatever it was that he had been doing, he clearly had not intended for anyone else to know about, much less see him doing it. His hands clenched into fists. He was looking at us, trying to decide what to do, I guess. He was outnumbered, but I don't think it made a difference – if he wanted to, he probably could have taken us. Maybe not won, but who knows. We also didn't know if he was wearing that bike chain around his waist like before.

He looked equal parts angry and guilty. There was something else though. He looked hurt. I remembered the pitcher we got kicked out of that game – it was like that. He abruptly turned around and ran towards the front, leaving me and Ricky standing there. I flicked the flashlight off.

I didn't know what he was trying to do out there with the lawn art and the candles and the midnight ceremonies, but I realized he was *serious*. It meant something to him. We had never considered that. He wasn't into any of the sports we were into, didn't hang out in the neighborhood with the rest of us (although to be fair that was kinda his own doing), and he had stopped riding bikes as far as we could tell. Maybe he needed something, and it was all he had. The more I thought about it the worse I felt. We should have just left it alone but instead we barged in with some stupid kids stuff. He didn't deserve that, and we didn't mean to go that far, but there was no going back now.

We were still just standing there not saying anything. I was too shocked; part of me couldn't understand what was happening at all. We had gone from certain death to I don't even know what. That look on his face though … I could feel it making a deep pit in my chest.

"We should get out of here," Ricky said flatly. He had seen his face too; I could tell by the tone of his voice.

"Yeah. Should we blow that candle out?"

"Yeah," Ricky took off the heavy metal wig and mask, bent down and blew out the candle.

"We gotta get Ant, he's still in the garage," I said. I still felt like whatever gears in my head that normally meshed were no longer doing that. James Barlow should have leapt on us like a raging bear. At least he would have in one reality, and that was apparently the reality we had just left, because where we were now, I had no explanations.

"What happened? Why did you turn on the light? I didn't know if I should go or not, that wasn't the signal," Ant was saying.

"We gotta get out of here, pack this stuff up, the whole thing is off, just forget it," Ricky said.

We were pulling down the wires and I was coiling up the rope, and Ricky was balling up the fabric after cutting it off the line. Ant had gone to get the boombox out of the garage and the remote walkie talkies on that side, we were handling the ones nearest us. It was all going smoothly, we just wanted to get it down and get out of there before we had to go and further contemplate the reality of what we had done. There was a rustle in the bushes at the corner of the yard, and what sounded like some huffing and puffing. Or grunting?

"Hey, did you hear that? Ant ... that you?" I whispered towards the sound. There was no reply. Ricky and I froze. What if James had doubled back already? It felt like we had packed everything up pretty quickly, but maybe James recovered faster than expected. Or changed his mind about fighting. We were trying to get a look at anything that might be in the bushes, but it was way too dark to see anything clearly over there and I was not about to risk using the flashlight again.

"Raccoons again?" Ricky whispered from behind

me.

"Maybe. Seems like it was big whatever it was. Wait…over there…." I pointed to the corner of the yard.

A shape that looked like it was made from shadows was separating itself from the bushes and overgrowth. It began to rise up until it was kid sized, then highschooler sized, then adult sized, and then it turned, and it had a face, a white expressionless face surrounded by what looked like a cloak of shifting shadow and night. And then it started closing the distance between us, quickly.

I was frozen. Something in my head just – I don't know, short circuited or reset or something. I literally could not move. I had not considered the possibility that James Barlow had been successful with his whatever it was he was doing, and perhaps whatever he had managed to summon was now back here on the loose.

"*PEACHES RUN*" Ricky was not petrified, and grabbed my arm, pulling me back towards the alley. That snapped me out of it, and then adrenaline and fear hit hard – so hard I bashed into the fence on the way out, but it hooked my shirt. I could feel something pulling on my shirt, and not realizing it was the fence I completely lost it and ran right out of my shirt. It ripped all the way up to the collar, which I tore off over my head and sprinted after Ricky, leaving my torn shirt hanging on the fence. I could feel whatever it was getting closer. We were going to have to make a stand out here in the alley, so we both stopped and got ready to meet our fate.

It was almost on top of where we were, and it was….

laughing?

"Hahaha..." came from behind us.

Wait a minute...

"Ah hahaha...." I knew that laugh too well, "Go home you dumbasses.... hahaha," said Mr. Kaminski from under his blank face mask. My ripped shirt came flying out into the alley, "Don't forget your shirt...hahahahaha, oh man..." and we heard him walking back through the bushes towards the front of the house. "And you guys leave that kid alone from now on. He's got enough troubles without you idiots getting involved. Mind your own business." We heard him walking back out front.

I went over and picked up my shirt from the ground. Ricky was bent over with his hands on his knees.

"What...just...was..that...ah jeeze man...."

We got *worked* by Mr. Kaminski. And badly. He must have seen that we were up to something. After all, we put a lot of it together in his back yard, and we didn't really pay him any mind because he never seemed to have more than a mild interest in what we did. In this case he acted like he wasn't paying much attention, but apparently, he was. I don't know what kind of info he had about James Barlow, but they were his next-door neighbors, he saw everything that was going on and he was pretty friendly with Mr. Barlow. I was angry and confused and impressed all at the same time.

It could have been worse though. We found out the next day that before he came after us he locked their garage door and killed the power, leaving Ant in the silent darkness while he was messing with us. It was maybe five minutes, but Ant said it felt like an hour. Then he held that creepy blank face mask up in front of the window like a floating head before letting Ant out, presumably to go change his shorts.

He had taught us a lesson though: there are unwritten rules for more than just baseball. Some of them are obvious, some you only find out about when you break them, or someone tells you. Or both. Mr. Kaminski was playing on an entirely different level than we were, and he was letting us know we had gone out of bounds in his own way.

Two days later, all the stuff was gone from the Barlows' yard. We didn't see him do it. We hadn't seen James at all since that night. Amy said he took it all down without any explanation, and also gave her back her diary and several other personal items he had taken, also without explanation. She didn't want to discuss it or much else with us either. I didn't blame her.

I don't know if it was worth it no matter how much we thought he deserved it. We never did anything like that again, it pretty much ended the secret agent stuff, ninja stuff, the booby traps and all that. It felt juvenile and pointless. We just lost our appetite for it.

When school started again, James wasn't there. There were rumors of drugs, rehab, divorce, bankruptcy, and some other more far-fetched theories, but it was all speculation. We had no way to verify anything, and we hadn't heard our parents mention anything about them either.

Two months later, the Barlows were gone. It was still before Thanksgiving when my brother and I saw a moving truck parked out front one morning on the way to school. By the time we got home it was gone and so were they. No explanation. There was a pile of garbage and boxes on the concrete pad where the garage had been, but none of us were brave enough to rummage through it. I don't know where they went, and we didn't see them around town anywhere. My brother said Amy was gone from school too and never said anything beforehand. Just gone. No realtor "For Sale" sign ever went up on the lawn, it was suddenly an empty house.

It stayed empty all winter as far as we could tell. And just as suddenly one Friday in April it wasn't. There was another moving truck, this time unloading. My brother and I were tossing a red and white plastic mini football we still had from the insurance agency back and forth when we walked past after school, and there was a girl sitting on the porch steps. She looked about my age.

"Heads up!" I said and tossed her the football. She caught it and tossed it back. "You moving in?" I asked.

"Yes."

"From….."

"Crown Point."

"Indiana? Wow, so new school and everything. Do you know anyone here?"

"No, but my mom says I should be excited at the opportunity to meet new people. Hurrah." She was one hundred percent *not* excited.

"Oh. Yeah. Sorry. It's not too bad here. Bunch of kids our age around anyway. We live right down there, the first two-flat," I said, pointing at our house.

"Ok. What's your name?" She asked.

For some reason I flashed back to the All-Star game announcer, *"Now bobbbbingggg for the Nerfsiiiibe tartars, Peebaaah Jupidahhhh,"* and it made me smirk. "I'm Pete." Peaches didn't feel quite right here.

"I'm Katie," she smiled back at me. She had a ponytail.

"Nice to meet you. This is my brother." I pointed my thumb at him and he waved. I went on, "It's a good neighborhood, your house is in the perfect spot, right in the middle of all the action."

"It's ok I guess. Can I ask you something?"

"Sure."

"Do you know why there are mirrors all over the living room and dining room walls in there?" she pointed her thumb over her shoulder, "It's weird. We're having them taken out, but I was just wondering if you knew anything about the people who used to live here."

"Well…it's kind of a long story. Let me run home and get out of these school clothes real quick and then I'll come back and fill you in?"

"OK cool." She was smiling a bit more now.

I tossed her the football, and then jogged home to change as quickly as I could.

WHAT HAPPENS NEXT

If you enjoyed *Our End Of The Block*, and are curious about what happens to Pete, Ricky, Katie, Ant and the rest of the bunch, you are in luck. This is part one of three; high school is next, and it's nothing like they expected. Visit pjjulius.com for the latest updates.

ABOUT THE AUTHOR

P.J. Julius grew up in the suburbs of Chicago, where he spent most of his time playing baseball, bike riding, playing guitar, and skateboarding. He's worked a variety of jobs in a variety of industries including manufacturing, finance, and advertising. He still enjoys playing guitar and bike riding.